Runaway Gran

RUNAWAY GRAN

by

Sonia Craddock

James Lorimer & Company Ltd., Publishers
Toronto

James Lorimer & Company Ltd. acknowledges the support of the Ontario Arts Council. We acknowledge the support of the Government of Canada through the Book Publishing Industry Development Program (BPIDP) for our publishing activities. We acknowledge the support of the Canada Council for the Arts for our publishing program. We acknowledge the support of the Government of Ontario through the Ontario Media Development Corporation's Ontario Book Initiative.

Series cover design: Iris Glaser Canada Council for the Arts   Conseil des Arts du Canada

ONTARIO ARTS COUNCIL
CONSEIL DES ARTS DE L'ONTARIO

Library and Archives Canada Cataloguing in Publication

Craddock, Sonia
[Rosemary for remembrance]
    Runaway Gran / Sonia Craddock.
(Streetlights)
First published in 1996 under title: Rosemary for remembrance.
ISBN-13: 978-1-55028-953-4
ISBN-10: 1-55028-953-5
    I. Title. II. Title: Rosemary for remembrance. III. Series.
PS8555.R24R67 2006   jC813'.54   C2006-903623-3

James Lorimer & Company Ltd., Publishers
317 Adelaide Street West
Suite 1002
Toronto, Ontario, M5V 1P9
www.lorimer.ca

Distributed in the
United States by:
Orca Book Publishers
P.O. Box 468
Custer, WA USA
98240-0468

Printed and bound in Canada.

For Grandad Ching and Barnaby's Granny.
With thanks to Loretta Kwan.

1

Runaway

MY GRAN RAN away on a Sunday. She ran away early in the morning on a showery Sunday in June. It had to be really early too because I get up as soon as it's daylight and I didn't see her at all.

***

I was wandering around the garden sniffing freshness. My bare feet felt icy as they soaked into the grass and I tracked spongy footprints across the lawn.

Dozens of diamond drops sparkled from the centre of the lupine leaves. They looked real as if I could pick them up and hold them in my hand.

"Rosy! Rosy!" Dad's voice boomed over the lawn. "Have you seen your grandmother?"

"What?" I called back. I reached out my little finger and touched one of the diamonds. It changed into plain rain water and ran down the stalk.

Dad came to the edge of the deck, wrapped his robe tightly around him as the sun disappeared behind a cloud and shouted louder. "Rosy, have you seen your grandmother this morning?"

"No," I yelled. I wished Dad wouldn't shout my name out like that. He was the only one who called me Rosy. The name was embarrassing enough, without the whole of Vancouver hearing it. But then, knowing Dad, I was lucky he didn't yell out a complete description to the world: Rosemary Green, eleven-year-old girl with bruises on her knees from playing floor hockey in the gym.

"Rosy, come inside," my dad bellowed loud enough to wake the neighbours for blocks around. "Your grandmother's disappeared."

"What do you mean?" I raced for the house, just as the rain started spitting down. "What do you mean, Dad? How can Gran have disappeared?"

Everyone, except Gran, was in the kitchen. The room was full of voices, and the smell of coffee and burnt toast.

"Guess what, Rose?" My eight-year-old sister met me at the door. "Gran's run away! Dad's phoning the police." She pushed her glasses back up her nose. "Maybe she's run away to a tropical island. I bet she's run away to Hawaii. Or maybe —"

"Shut up, Goldy!" I shoved her aside.

"What's going on? What's happened to Gran?" I slipped into the chair next to my grandad.

"Your gran seems to have disappeared, Rose," said Grandad, as he sipped his coffee.

"But, Grandad!" I didn't understand this. Grandad was drinking his coffee, as if he wasn't worried at all. If my gran had disappeared, why wasn't my grandad more upset?

"How can Gran have disappeared?" My giant six-foot-seven brother, Basil, hooted from across the table. "She's eighty-five. You just don't disappear when you're that old." He crunched away at a bowl of cereal. "You don't run down the street and jump on a bus. The odds of that happening must be millions to one."

"Let's just keep calm," said Grandad.

"Well, the police haven't seen her and she's not at any of the hospitals." Dad dropped the phone with a clatter and pulled at his beard. "And she hasn't taken her handbag or a coat, so maybe she's just somewhere nearby."

"Dad! Dad!" Goldy tugged at his arm. "If Gran hasn't run away to Hawaii, I bet she's been kidnapped! I bet she's been kidnapped by a gang."

"Kidnapped!" Dad grabbed her shoulder. "What do you mean? Don't talk nonsense."

"It isn't nonsense!" Goldy scowled. "It isn't." She stared at us. "Maybe Gran looked out the window and saw a man and recognized him and he had to kidnap her to keep her quiet. Maybe he was a member of one of those gangs we heard about on TV last week. Maybe —"

"Do be quiet, Marigold," Dad said. "We're trying to think."

I snorted. No one in their right mind would think that Gran had been kidnapped, or gran-napped, I guess I should say.

"I would estimate the chances of Gran being kidnapped at about one in a billion." Basil balanced his cereal bowl on one finger, twirled it around and stashed it in the dishwasher. "I say we're wasting time. Shouldn't we be out looking for her?"

"Of course we should." Dad stood up. "Iris, you drive around the neighbourhood."

My older sister Iris didn't answer. She was hunched in her chair, nibbling on burnt toast, lost in a chemistry textbook.

"Iris!" Dad grabbed the book from her plate. "Do listen!"

"I *am* listening." Iris smiled up at him, her long black hair tangled around her face. "Maybe we should phone the police. They might have seen Gran."

Dad sighed. "I've done that, Iris. I want you to get the truck and look for Gran."

"Maybe we should phone the hospitals too," said Iris.

"I've done that as well." Dad's voice rose a bit.

"I'll get my bike and go round the park."

Basil bent down and tied the laces on his enormous basketball shoes. "The odds are that she's close by."

"Er, yes ... I'll walk around the block and talk to the neighbours." Dad hurriedly pushed his T-shirt into his jeans. "Mrs. Dunk may have seen her."

Basil groaned. "Mrs. Dunk! Dunk the skunk, you mean. She's always drenched in that stinky perfume."

That was true. Mrs. Dunk is a very nosy neighbour who doesn't like kids. She has a yappy Chihuahua, called Pepi, who she keeps tucked under her arm like a handbag.

"Wait! I want to go with you, Dad," said Goldy. "I'll get dressed." She rushed out of the kitchen.

"Rosy! You and your grandfather stay here in case of a phone call." Dad pulled his beard again and rushed out of the room too.

So that left Grandad and me.

"When did you notice that Gran had gone?" I

dragged my chair nearer to him and poured myself some Cheerios into a bowl. My grandad has trouble hearing and seeing, and I thought maybe there was a chance he'd just overlooked her. Sometimes he doesn't turn on his hearing-aid and misses all sorts of things.

"Six o'clock this morning." Grandad sipped his coffee and made a face. "I woke up and your grandmother wasn't there." He nodded. "Her side of the bed was cold too. I felt the sheets."

"Did you look for her? I mean she might be in the house somewhere." I still couldn't understand why my grandad didn't seem worried.

"First thing I thought of, Rose. Of course I did. And so did your dad. We searched the whole house, even under the beds."

The thought of my tiny grandmother crawling under the beds to hide made me smile.

Vroom! Vroom! Vroom! The noise of an accelerator burst into the room, and I ran to the window. "Iris has the gears stuck again."

I watched our battered green truck jerk its way down the hill and around the corner. It had

"Green Thumb Gardeners" in flaking yellow letters across the side. The truck was so old it broke down nearly every day, but Dad said we didn't have any money to fix it properly, let alone buy a new one.

Grandad gave a little moan.

I nodded sympathetically and patted his arm. Grandad lost his driving licence because of something called depth perception. When you get old, you have to have a medical certificate to keep driving and the doctor told Grandad that it was "no go."

"Now, Rose," said Grandad and he drained the last of his cold coffee. "Since I can't drive the truck, we'd better phone for a taxi."

"A taxi!"

"Yes. You know what a taxi is." He grinned at me and straightened his tie.

"But we're suppose to stay here in case the phone rings." I stared at him. "Why do you want a taxi?"

"Because I know where your gran is," he said calmly.

2

Bad Day (BD) and
Very Bad Day (VBD)

"You know where Gran is?" I tripped over the words. "But, where? And why didn't you say?"

"Because your father would get worried and start shouting, and I don't want your gran upset."

That was true. When my father got worried, he always shouted, and the person he worried about most was definitely Gran. So I phoned for a taxi.

***

"Take us to 888 Arbutus Avenue," Grandad told the taxi driver as we sank back into the seats of the yellow cab.

"But Grandad!" I said. "That's —"

"Home. Your gran's gone home. That's where I think she's gone."

"But it's not her home! Her home is here."

"Arbutus Avenue was our home for sixty-five years," Grandad reminded me softly.

I looked out the window. Large drops of rain were spotting the glass. I couldn't even begin to imagine sixty-five years; eleven years was enough. But I think I could imagine how I might feel about having to leave my home after such a long, long time. I had never thought about it before. I was so pleased that Gran and Grandad had moved in with us that I never imagined they might not feel the same way.

"Is Gran unhappy with us? Doesn't she like her room? She could have the room that Goldy and I share, if that would help."

I hated sharing a room with Goldy. Dad said it was only temporary but temporary had been nearly two years. I'd do anything to change rooms.

"She's not unhappy because of the family or

the room." Grandad paused. "Your gran is just having some VBDs."

"Very bad days, not just bad days?" I said quickly.

Grandad nodded.

***

Two years ago my Mum got very sick and had to go to the hospital. Gran and Grandad came to look after us. They left their own house empty. They thought they were only going to stay for a little while, but then Mum died. It was a black, terrible time. It was such a black time that I don't even want to think about it, and Dad got so depressed that he stopped working. For months he just hung around the house in his robe and did nothing. Lots of days he didn't even get out of bed. So Gran and Grandad had to stay with us. Grandad was eighty-nine, but he had to start work again and try to keep our family business, Green Thumb Gardeners, going. Gran and Grandad sold their house and used up all their money; but even though Dad got better and started working as hard as he could, Green Thumb Gardeners is practically bankrupt. We are broke, and everyone worries about money.

It's been nearly two years since Mum died, but I still dream about her a lot. It's always the same dream. I'm sitting in our cedar tree looking at the freighters anchored in English Bay, and Mum is weeding in her herb garden below me.

"How many freighters are out there, Rose?" she asks.

"Twelve," I say, counting them slowly. But that doesn't seem right. "No, eleven." But that doesn't seem right either. "Twenty ... seventeen." I keep counting again and again to try and get the same number, but I never can.

In the morning when I wake up the first thing that comes into my head is the freighters.

"Mum!" I call, as I jump out of bed. "I've had a crazy dream!" And then I remember ... It hurts to remember, so I try my hardest not to, but I can't help it. It's strange, but I'm trying all I can to lose memories, while my gran is trying all she can to keep them.

My gran's memory is slowly getting worse and worse. For instance, last summer my great aunt Josephine died too — only she was eighty-three years old. She was Gran's favourite sister. Gran flew to San Francisco for Great Aunt Josephine's funeral, but when she came back she forgot she was living with us and took the taxi back to Arbutus Avenue, her old house, which was up for sale.

Gran got very upset and phoned Dad. "Something terrible has happened," she told him. "There's a 'For Sale' sign on the lawn of my house. And Arthur (that's my grandad) isn't here! You'd better phone the police!"

"You're in the wrong house, Mother," Dad said. "Rosy and I will come and get you."

So, Dad and I had to drive across Vancouver to get Gran and when we arrived at her old house, she had her coat off and she was dusting, like she still lived there!

Well, after that. Gran's memory began to go up and down like a roller coaster. Some days it was fine, and some days it wasn't. And then, a month or so ago, Gran started to have bad days when she got everything totally muddled up. Grandad calls these days BDs for short.

"BD today," he'll say, when I get home from school. And that means that all Gran will talk about will be money and she won't know who anyone is. From some reason. Gran always thinks I'm her sister Josephine.

"Oh, Josephine," she says to me. "I'm so glad you're here. Please give me some money. I need money."

But other days Grandad gives me a thumbs-up and says, "GD today. Rose."

"Rose!" Gran calls out. I'll run into the kitchen, and we'll hug each other.

"How was school?" she asks me. "Did that mean Mr. Tremblay keep you in again? I've a good mind to go to that school and give him the sharp end of my tongue!" Gran and Grandad and I laugh and joke. GDs are like a present.

The funny thing is that I don't even mind the BDs. It's like Gran is part of something that no one can control, like the weather. Some days it's sunny and some days it's rainy, and that's that. No one can control the weather.

Gran can't control her BDs and GDs. In fact, Grandad said she doesn't even know that she has BDs, so she's not unhappy.

The person who is unhappy is Dad.

"But, Mother, I'm your son," he says over and over, when Gran has a BD and doesn't know him. He tries everything he can to get Gran to remember him. He gets out all the photo albums and sits next to her and points at the pictures of himself.

"Here's me sitting on your lap," he tells her. "Here's me getting first prize in grade one. Here's me swimming in the ocean. Here's me at scout camp. Here's me at my graduation. Here's me getting married." That picture makes him cry. Then he points at his face. "Here's me now, your son, Brian, fifty-five years old."

The strange thing is that Gran recognizes some of the photos.

"Brian!" she says, when she sees the picture of Dad in his scout uniform. "Brian."

Gran recognizes Dad in all the photos, up to about twenty years ago. Dad spreads all the photos in a line, and she recognizes him all the way up to the photo taken right after he grew a beard.

"Maybe it's the beard," says Dad. "Maybe you don't recognize me with the beard, Mother."

So Dad shaved off his beard — but it didn't help. Gran still didn't recognize him or the photos of the last twenty years. Shaving his beard off just made Dad look weird for a month until it grew back again.

Dad gets terribly upset that Gran can't remember him on her BDs, as if he isn't important enough to crash through her memory gaps.

But that isn't all. Gran doesn't just forget Dad, she forgets all sorts of things. She puts the kettle on the stove, turns the element up high — and forgets it. She starts to iron clothes and then goes away and leaves the iron on. She turns on the taps and forgets to turn them off.

After Gran flooded the kitchen and basement, Dad got Iris, Basil, Goldy, and me together.

"I want you to watch Gran all the time," he said. "I'm very worried that Gran will hurt herself."

"We do try!" I told Dad. "But Gran doesn't want to be looked after. She hates us taking over. She doesn't like us cooking dinner, and she keeps shooing us out of the kitchen."

"Well, at least lay the table. Rosy," Dad told me. "That way we won't have to eat with serving spoons."

I don't know why anyone would fuss when Gran lays the table with the wrong spoons.

"It doesn't bother me," I said. "I don't care what sort of spoons we eat with."

"I do," said Goldy. "I can't get those big spoons in my mouth." She stuck her tongue out. "See. I bruised my tongue!"

"Who cares," I said, and I pulled horror faces at her until she started whining.

"Dad! Tell Rose to stop." She went and hid behind Dad's back.

"And make sure Gran doesn't put the plates in the freezer." Dad gave me a meaningful look. "You can do that."

I couldn't see why it mattered if Gran put the plates in the freezer. It didn't bother me. But it sure worried Dad, and even Basil and Goldy muttered. Iris never noticed anything, so you couldn't count her.

Grandad doesn't worry either. He says he just waits to see what each day brings.

I do too. Last Thursday Gran got time totally muddled and when we sat down for dinner we got quite a surprise.

"Porridge!" Goldy said in a sort of yelping voice, when Gran dished up oatmeal and brown sugar.

Gran smiled at us. "I do like a good breakfast," she said. "It starts the day off right."

And then on Friday morning Gran gave us stew for breakfast. I don't mind if Gran muddles time. Who says you can't have stew for breakfast anyway? Even if it is mostly beans with hardly any meat.

***

Now Grandad was telling me that Gran had gone back to their old house — which was sold a year ago — and that she was having a VBD, something he'd never mentioned before.

"Gran is having a Very Bad Day?"

"Yes."

"What does that mean?"

"Your Gran keeps talking about a box. A missing box." Grandad rubbed the steam off the taxi window and stared out. We were crossing Lion's Gate Bridge. The water was grey and choppy far below, and a giant white cruise ship was gliding past, probably on its way to Alaska.

"Yes, a missing box," Grandad repeated.

"Quite a mystery."

I hadn't heard about this. "What sort of box?"

"I don't know. Your Gran didn't say except she thinks the box will save us somehow! And yesterday she kept on and on about it. First she looked all round the house. She searched everywhere. Then last night she told me she had to go back home to get it — to her proper home. I sort of put her off. I thought maybe today she ..."

"Yes, I know," I said. "But today wasn't a GD?"

"Guess not. Guess she woke up in the middle of the night and decided to go by herself. That's what I'm figuring."

"And Gran thinks this box will save us?" I was puzzled. "What does she mean?"

"She says it's to do with money. Save us from being broke."

"Gran worries about money all the time," I said. I worried too, but not all the time.

"Yes. Maybe she thinks her box is valuable. That's my guess," said Grandad. "But I've never seen any box," he said, almost to himself.

It's a long way to Arbutus Avenue from our house. We live in a district of Vancouver called Kitsilano, five blocks from English Bay. From our deck we can actually see Gran and Grandad's old house, across the water, but to get there we have to drive all the way to West Vancouver. It took the taxi thirty-five minutes.

The taxi was very expensive. I kept looking at the meter.

"Don't worry, Rose. I've got an emergency fund," said Grandad. He must have guessed what I was thinking.

"If Gran is here in your old house," I said, as we finally pulled to a stop. "How do you think she got here?"

"I don't know," said Grandad.

"Well, she couldn't walk this far," I said. "And she doesn't have her handbag with her, so she hasn't got bus fare."

"Certainly a mystery," said Grandad.

When we got out of the taxi, the rain was really belting down and the North Shore mountains had disappeared behind grey clouds.

We scurried up the wet path to the front door of 888 Arbutus Avenue. Grandad rang the bell. I remembered the chimes — they sounded like Big Ben. The door had been painted a fresh new blue. On either side of the porch were shiny brown pots with golden dragons wrapped around them. They were filled with red geraniums.

"Very nice," said Grandad. He approved of geraniums.

Then we heard footsteps hurrying to the door. The lock was turned, and the door opened.

3

Total Strangers

"HELLO!" SAID A voice. " I hope you're not selling anything. I don't have any money."

Grandad and I just stood with our mouths open and stared.

It was Gran, and she looked just like her usual self, with her yellowy-white curls and her blue fleece suit.

"Cessy!" said Grandad. "Cessy, are you all right?"

My gran, whose real name is Cecilia, frowned a bit and looked puzzled. "Do I know you?" she said.

Then I knew it was a VBD because Gran always knows Grandad — even when she forgets Dad and me and the others.

"Well," said Grandad, very softly, "we've been married for sixty-five years. I'm Arthur."

Gran stared at him for a long time. "You look very old," she said doubtfully. "My Arthur is a handsome man."

"Well," said Grandad again, with a small smile, "I've aged a lot in the last few hours."

Then Gran looked at me, and a smile lit up her face. "Josephine!" She clapped her hands.

"How lovely. What a surprise. I thought you were in San Francisco! You've come to help me find the box."

I stepped forward and gave her a big hug. My little gran is so thin her bones feel like a bird's, and I'm as tall as she is. "Hi, Cessy," I smiled at her. If she calls me Josephine, I call her Cessy so she won't get more confused. "It's great to see you too," I said. If my gran wants me to be Josephine, it's fine by me. "Sure I'll help you. What does the box look like?"

"I don't know." Gran looked at me with a worried expression. "I thought you knew, Josephine. Don't you remember? You gave it to me."

"I did?" I said.

"The box is so important. I must have my box!" Gran twisted her hands over and over, as if she was trying to knot her memory together. "It will save us."

I didn't know what to say. I looked at Grandad, but he just smiled and shrugged his shoulders.

"Can we come in, Cessy?" Grandad asked.

"Of course. Of course. What am I thinking of, you must be soaking wet." Gran gave Grandad another puzzled look. "Are you sure you're Arthur?"

"Quite sure," Grandad said firmly.

I felt really weird walking into the house. I mean, where were the people who lived there? I couldn't understand how my gran had reached the house in the first place, let alone got inside! "Let's go!" I whispered to Grandad. "Let's get Gran and go right now!" I wanted to run before we were caught.

But Grandad didn't hear me.

"Give me those wet jackets!" Gran hovered in

the hall, as if it were her own house. "I'll hang them up."

The hall looked the same as always. The oak coat stand with its black iron hooks, wavy mirror and a metal tray at the bottom for dripping umbrellas still stood in the same place. I looked into the mirror to see if it still made my nose look crooked. It did.

Gran hung up our wet jackets and led the way into the living room. "Strange things have been happening." She waved her arms around.

"The paint has changed colour. And there is a lot of new furniture." She pointed at the chairs, chests and tables that were arranged around the room. "It's very strange." She looked puzzled again.

I glanced at my Grandad. Sitting in a comfy armchair, he seemed as though he hadn't a care in the world.

"Grandad!" I whispered. "What if someone comes? I think we should go." Any moment a great big man, or a whole family, could come bursting in and catch us. It's against the law to break into houses. They'd be sure to phone the police.

"There's something else that's very strange." Gran nodded towards the kitchen. "There's a strange woman in there."

I knew it. I knew we were going to get caught.

"Grandad!" I hissed loudly at him. "Quick! Let's run for it!" And I started for the front door.

"It's all right, Rose." Grandad's voice was as calm and soft as always. He pulled himself out of the chair. "Let's go meet this strange woman, shall we?"

"I don't know what she's doing in my house. She won't answer when I talk to her." Gran shook her white curls sadly. "I think we're going to have to call the police."

"Maybe we should wait a bit," Grandad said mildly "No rush."

I gulped. No rush. I should say not.

Sitting at the corner of the nook in the kitchen, her hands clasped together and looking very scared indeed, was a tiny woman dressed in black trousers and a tunic with her grey hair pinned up in a bun at the back of her neck.

Someone else's gran. Someone else's Chinese gran.

"You see!" said my gran.

"Oh dear," said Grandad.

"She's a total stranger!" Gran said accusingly.

The tiny woman looked up at us all, from where she was huddled at the end of the table, and then looked quickly down again, as though we would disappear, if only she didn't see us.

"Hmm." Grandad cleared his throat. "Dear lady, please forgive us. I'm very sorry about the intrusion. Please don't be alarmed. We mean you no harm."

"Grandad, I don't think she understands English," I told him.

"No. Maybe not," he said. "But she understands my tone of voice. It's not always the words that count."

I couldn't see this myself, but he seemed to be right because the woman lifted her head and stared at him with deep black eyes.

Grandad bowed his head at her and smiled, and after a pause the lady gave a very tiny smile back and bowed to him. At this I took a deep breath and collapsed onto the padded bench of the nook. I felt as though I hadn't breathed in hours. My legs were all rubbery.

Then the tiny lady nodded and smiled at me, and I nodded and smiled back at her. And then we were all nodding and smiling at one another. Even Gran got into the act, but she looked very puzzled. And then the lady started to talk rapidly to us in a high musical voice. Of course we didn't understand a word, but we all smiled some more, and Grandad was quite right. It's the tone that counts.

I guess we might have sat for quite a long time just smiling and nodding and looking around the room, which hadn't changed much at all except for a row of black metal woks hanging on one wall, piles of bamboo steamers on the tops of the cupboards, and a different smell of spices. We might have sat for hours, but suddenly there was the sound of a car door slamming, footsteps running up the back steps — and the screen door crashed open.

4

Police!

"GRANDMOTHER! I'M HOME! *Po, po, ni zai ma*?" A young man in jeans and a white shirt, carrying a pile of textbooks, came rushing into the kitchen.

"Oh!" He stopped dead as he saw us all sitting around the kitchen nook. "Hi!"

"Hi!" said Grandad, smiling.

"Who are you?" said Gran.

"*Zhe shi wo waisun*," said the Chinese grandmother. "John." She pointed at the man. "John."

I said nothing. I just closed my eyes and tried to pretend I wasn't there.

"I'm John Chan." The man put his books down on the table. "If you're here to see my parents, I'm afraid they're out of town this weekend, at a lawyer's convention. They won't be back until this evening."

"No, we're not here to see your parents," Grandad told him. "It's a bit more complicated than that."

I'll say! I couldn't think how Grandad was going to explain.

John looked at us and grinned. "I'm surprised my grandmother let you inside. She's only been here a few weeks from Hong Kong and she's very nervous." He turned to his grandmother and spoke quickly in Chinese.

The little lady shook her head at him and pointed at Gran. She began to talk very fast with a voice that sounded like a harp strumming. She sounded very excited.

In the middle of this conversation Gran suddenly got up and started opening cupboards.

"My box! My box!" she said. She opened and shut one cupboard after another. "It must be here," she said. "My box is here somewhere. I must find it. I must find it."

"*Bu shi ya!*" The Hong Kong gran got up too

and ran over to her and shut the doors fast. Gran opened them again.

"Stop it!" Gran said loudly and pulled at the Chinese gran's sleeve. "Arthur?" She turned around and looked at my Grandad doubtfully.

"Arthur, I really think this lady's grandson should take her home."

"*Ni zuo xia!*" The Chinese gran pulled her sleeve away.

"Stop!" Grandad and John said together, and John bounded across the room and stood between the two grannies, who were glaring at one another.

***

I thought it would take ages for the explanations to sort themselves out — and it did. John Chan's grandmother had got really scared when Gran just opened the kitchen door, walked right inside the house, and started opening cupboards. John was at college, and she thought that maybe it was some strange Western custom. When John finished explaining to her, she made a soft tutting sound, hurried over to my gran, bowed at her and opened all the cupboards along the counters.

"*Jia ma da de po po, ni keyi kaw kaw na qui zi*," she said, bowing and smiling to Gran.

They were both the same height.

"What did she say?" asked Grandad.

"She says the Canadian grandmother can look in all the cupboards she wants to." John grinned.

"She is sympathetic. She, too, lives in her children's house now." He grinned wider. "My grandmother does not always see eye to eye with my mother. They have different ways of doing things. Even though my parents were born in Hong Kong, they've been in Canada for nearly twenty years and they're very Western. There are many things my grandmother doesn't understand."

Grandad nodded.

Gran, who was very quiet while all this was going on, now moved to the hall door.

"I'm so tired." She gave a little yawn. "I think I'll go and have a lie down." She smiled politely at

John and his grandmother, as if they had just come to tea. "It was nice meeting you," she told them. "Come and visit again some time."

"Come on, Grandad!" I ran over and took my gran's arm. Now Gran was going to be like Goldilocks. We could be there all day. And what if Gran refused to leave? Mr. and Mrs. Chan would be bound to phone the police! The thought of my gran down at the police station, maybe even locked in a cell, made my heart thud.

"Well, Cessy," said Grandad, "I don't think that's such a good idea." He turned to John. "I wonder if we could ask you to phone for a taxi."

"I'll be pleased to give you a ride," John said. "If you don't mind a Jeep."

I didn't mind. I didn't mind if John had a garbage truck! But how were we going to get Gran to agree?

"The rain has stopped, and the sun is shining." Grandad went up to Gran and offered her his arm. "And John would like to take us for a little ride in his car."

I held my breath.

But it was all right! Gran smiled and took hold of Grandad's arm as if he was asking her for a dance, and we all nodded and bowed at Mrs. Chan — and left.

I'd never been in a Jeep before. A Jeep is much more fun than a car or a truck. I got to sit in the back with the spray from the wet road spitting all around me. And all the way home I wondered about how Gran had returned to her old house without any money. It was a real mystery. But, I didn't see how I could solve it. If I asked Gran while she was having a BD, she wouldn't know what I was talking about and if I asked her while she was having a GD she wouldn't remember.

***

I saw the flashing red light when we were a block from home. Police. Outside our house.

"Oh, oh!" said Grandad. "Looks like trouble."

It sure did. Dad was on the sidewalk talking to two policemen. He was waving his arms around and pointing wildly. Goldy was waving her arms around and pointing too. Our neighbour, Mrs. Dunk, with her yappy dog, Pepi, almost strangled under her arm, was staring at them all.

"Just drive past," Grandad said quickly to John Chan, and he pulled his jacket over his ears and hunched his head down. "Can't stand all that explaining."

John changed gears and drove sedately around the police car.

We'd have got away with it too if Gran hadn't chosen that moment to look straight into Dad's eyes. He shouted and raced after us.

So we had to stop and back up, and that was that. Caught!

"What happened?" Dad hurried frantically over to us. "Where did you go? I called the police. And what are you doing in that Jeep? What's going on?"

"We thought you'd been kidnapped too," Goldy said. She looked very disappointed.

"No one was kidnapped," I jumped out of the back of the Jeep.

"Well, where were you then?" Dad fussed. "Goldy and I came home and the house was empty. First my mother disappeared and then my father and a daughter." He ran his fingers through his beard, which looked like tangled string. "And then you all appear in a souped-up army car, with a stranger!" He glared at John suspiciously.

"It was weird!" Goldy gave a shiver. She is such an actor. "The house felt so deserted and scary. I told Dad about that movie we saw on TV the other night, you know, the one where the people all disappeared one by one and —"

"Do we take it that the lost persons are now found?" One of the policemen cut into Goldy's sentence. He too seemed a bit peeved that we hadn't been abducted. He was very tall and thin, and he swayed on his toes like a reed. I watched his shadow sway blackly behind him, as if it was in sympathy. His partner was only half his size and didn't sway at all, but then he was closer to the ground.

"Oh, yes, officers, they are," said Dad. "Thanks for coming. I'm sorry I called you unnecessarily."

He followed the policemen back to their car, apologizing all the way.

"Where's Iris?" I asked Goldy "And Basil? Have they been kidnapped too?"

"Funny! They're still out looking for Gran. And guess what?" She hopped up and down and giggled. "The policemen are called Jesse and James! Get it! Jesse James!" Goldy laughed, and her glasses fell off. Her glasses were all spotted, and one arm was stuck on with masking tape. I could tell she'd dressed in a hurry. She was wearing one green sock and one blue one, and her pink shirt was buttoned wrong.

"How do you know?" I grabbed her round the neck. "You're such a liar."

"Get off!" She pushed me away. "I asked them their names. The tall one's Jesse and the short one is James."

"I bet they're just kidding you." She sure got worked up over things.

Goldy sniffed. She hated to be doubted. She turned and stared at the Jeep, where John and Grandad were helping Gran out the narrow door.

"Where did you find the guy and the Jeep? And where was Gran?"

"It's a long story." I wasn't sure I wanted to tell her. "Too bad Gran came back so quickly," she said. "If she was still lost the police dogs could have tracked her. It would have been like a TV show."

I didn't answer her. Goldy thinks everything is like a TV show.

"And the TV people would interview us as well," said Goldy. But then she pulled a face. "I wish we had better names. Just because Dad loves plants doesn't mean he had to give us all plant names."

"Hmm," I said. I didn't mind being named Rosemary because it was my mother's name too. But I wished I could stop Dad calling me Rosy.

5

A Terrible Discovery

"SHE WENT HOME!" my father said incredulously. "Mother went all the way back to the old house on Arbutus Avenue! How did she get there?"

"I don't know how she got there, Brian," Grandad answered softly. "I've just told you that."

It was much later. Gran had gone to bed, and the rest of us were sitting on the deck eating nachos and cheese and watching the sun sink into the rim of the ocean.

"Red sky at night, gardener's delight," chanted Basil, and I saw tears come to his eyes. I felt a lump in my throat. It hurt, and I swallowed hard. Goldy climbed onto Dad's lap.

"Red sky at night, gardener's delight," is what Mum used to say when we watched the sunset. A red sky meant the next day was supposed to be sunny and that meant Dad wouldn't have to do people's gardens in the pouring rain and come home all wet and shivery.

"It's a lovely evening," said Grandad. He smiled at everyone, and when Grandad smiled, everyone smiled back. So it was all right. It was a good supper too, the sort of supper I liked best. Goldy hated nachos, so I ate all hers, plus my own share. Iris often forgot to eat, so I sat next to her and helped finish hers as well.

"I bet Gran is angry because there's never any hot water for her bath." Goldy looked across the deck at Basil who was bouncing a basketball between his legs. Whenever Basil was around I noticed that the whole space seemed filled up with just him.

"Hey! That is not fair," he said. "It's a calumny. I don't take all the hot water."

"Huh?" Goldy made a face at me. I shrugged. I didn't know what he meant. Sometimes Basil used big words just to confuse us.

"Yes, you do." Goldy wouldn't give up. "Every morning you shower for an hour."

Goldy exaggerated as usual, but she was right about Basil taking all the hot water.

"No, no," said Grandad. "That's not it. Your gran has her bath in the afternoon. It's me who has to have the cold shower." But he smiled at Basil as he said it.

My grandad has to be the nicest man in the whole world.

"Anyway," Basil reached across the deck to grab his ball, "I would say that listening to Rose's music would be far more likely to make a person run away. All that head banging and booming all day long."

I sprang forward and grabbed the basketball from Basil's hand. "I don't play loud music, do I, Iris?" I bounced the ball around her.

" I never hear it," she told me.

"Oh, Iris, you never hear anything," Basil said, grinning at her and trying to grab my ankle.

"The whole house could be collapsing and you wouldn't hear it."

I fell to the deck and wrapped my arms round the ball. Basil started poking me with his toe. "Oh, stop it!" Dad clapped his hands. "This is getting us nowhere. And put that ball away!"

He moved his feet from getting crushed, as I wriggled under his legs.

I wonder if your mother happened to meet someone she knew and got a ride that way."

Grandad turned to Dad. "Could have been as simple as that."

"I bet it was ETs from outer space." Goldy jumped around. "Just like in that science fiction movie we saw. Remember? There were two aliens who looked just like real humans and they captured people and took their brains."

"Goldy!" Basil grabbed her from behind. "Do stop making up stories. This is not the time."

"I'm not! I'm —" Goldy began stubbornly.

"Marigold!" Dad cut her off and turned back to Grandad. "But why would Mother go to the old house? It's been sold for over a year now."

"Well, you know your mother's memory isn't the best anymore," Grandad said gently. "She thinks she has lost some sort of a box. I think that's why she went back to the old house ... to try and find this box."

"What box?" Dad looked puzzled.

"I don't know." Grandad shrugged. "Your mother can't remember what it looks like or where it is. She's been looking everywhere. It seems very important to her."

"I heard Gran say that if she found her box we'd have a lot of money," Goldy said loudly. "What does she mean?"

"She thinks the box is valuable," I said. "She says it will save us."

"Well, you know how your Gran worries about money," Grandad said.

"We're all worried about money," said Dad with a sigh, and he rubbed his hand over his face, like he was very tired. "What does she think? Does she think she's got a box hidden somewhere that's full of one-thousand-dollar bills? She's dreaming!"

Goldy and I looked at one another. I knew what she was thinking. A box of one-thousand-dollar bills would save us. We could pay Green Thumb's debts. We'd be able to buy new clothes, and I could get my hair cut.

"It's a good dream," said Basil. "I like to imagine things like that myself. I dream I win the lottery or save a very rich man from drowning."

I stared at Basil. I never guessed he'd imagine stuff like that. I did all the time, but I thought only kids imagined such things. Basil was seventeen!

Dad sighed. "We're very lucky that the woman who lives in the house didn't phone the police."

I left them all talking and went and swung from the hand rail on the steps. I didn't want to worry anymore.

I swung back and forth and stared into the night. It had just started to sprinkle again, but I could still see lights shining in long glittering strings out of the silhouettes of the North Shore mountains. They were the lights from the ski lifts. When I was eight, I'd started to learn to ski, but now of course there wasn't any money for ski lessons. Dad said, "No way." He said that about everything. No skiing, no holidays, no camp, no mountain bike, no new clothes. I didn't mind about the skiing and I didn't mind about camp, but I really needed a new pair of runners. I peered down at my left foot and wiggled my toes. I could see my big toe sticking out, but I couldn't ask Dad for new ones. He got so upset when you asked him for money.

The steps creaked, and Goldy bounced down and clung to my T-shirt. "You're supposed to come in and get ready for bed. Dad is making our lunches."

"Cut that out!" I hung with one hand and pulled my shirt away. I'd forgotten it was school tomorrow.

Goldy kicked her feet against the railing. "Did you know that Gran might have to go and live in a nursing home?"

"What?" I dropped to the ground and stared up at her. "I don't believe you. You're such a liar." It couldn't be true. She had to be lying. Goldy was always making up stories.

"It's true. I heard Dad talking to someone on the phone. Dad thinks Gran needs looking after. He said she needs special care."

"We *are* looking after Gran," I said sharply. "Gran is just fine."

"I know." Goldy slipped down the last step and grabbed my knees. "But Dad is worried she'll get run over or hurt herself."

I shoved her away, hard. "I don't believe you!"

I shouted the words at her. "No way!" It couldn't be true. "How could Dad even think of such a thing!"

"It is true," Goldy said crossly. "And something else I heard, but I'm not telling you."

"What?"

"I'm not saying. You're mean to me."

"Tell me! Tell me now, or I'll sit on your head."

"No!"

I grabbed hold of her and twisted her down.

"Now tell!" I pinned her arms to her side. "Tell."

"Bully!" She spat at me.

I ducked, but I didn't let go of her, even though a gob of spit landed in my hair.

"All right." Goldy kicked out at me. "I'll tell— only let me up."

I let her go, and she rubbed her arms like I'd tortured her.

"I heard Dad say that it would cost such a lot of money for Gran to be kept in a nursing home that we'd have to sell the house." She looked at me. "I did hear that. I'm not lying, honest."

I believed her. Even Goldy wouldn't make up anything like that.

"If Dad sells the house, we'll have to sleep on the streets." Goldy twirled around on the step. "I saw a program about people living on the streets — or we could make a little hut under one of the bridges."

"Shut up!" I pushed past her and hurried inside.

6

It Can't Be True

"DAD! DAD! WHERE are you?" I yelled.

Dad was sitting at the Green Thumb business desk in the alcove off the dining room. The desk was covered in piles and piles of paper, and the computer was making weird peeping noises.

When Mum was alive, she used to do the book-keeping for the company, and everything was neat and tidy. Now it's just a big mess.

Even though I was right next to him. Dad didn't hear me. He was muttering to himself. "Bill! Bills! Bills!" I heard him say.

"Dad!" I pulled at his arm. "Dad! Goldy told me —"

"Not now, Rosy." Dad grabbed a fistful of

envelopes in one hand and started banging at the computer keys with the other. "I'm busy. I can't talk now."

"But I want to ask you —"

"Please, not now!" Dad's voice rose. "I've got an appointment at the credit union on Saturday. I'm going to ask for a loan, but first I've got to get all the accounts straight."

"But Dad!"

"Rosy! Don't bother me!" Dad's face was getting red. I could tell he was about to start shouting, so I left.

***

I decided to ask Iris about Gran. I went into her room and flung myself on her bed.

"Goldy says she heard Dad talking about putting Gran in a nursing home." I watched Iris open a textbook and settle down at her desk. I could hardly even say the words out loud.

"It's not true, is it?"

"I haven't heard that," Iris murmured.

"Dad thinks Gran might hurt herself. He thinks she needs special care."

Mmm. Well, that might be true. Gran would get more care in a nursing home." She took off an elastic band and shook her hair free.

"You don't mean that!" I sat up and stared at her. "Don't you care if Gran has to go away?" I couldn't believe her. "Don't you love Gran?"

Iris spun her chair round and faced me.

"Rose, shhh ... don't get so upset. It may never happen."

"Don't you care?" I asked again.

"Of course I do!" She bent her head forward." But there's no use worrying about it," she said as she twisted her hair into a braid.

"If you cared, you'd do something." I felt a scream like a hard lump rising inside me, and I clenched my fists as hard as I could, so it wouldn't burst out.

"Rose, Gran is eighty-five years old. You know what that means. It means she's going to die soon. So is Grandad. He's ninety-one. So will we when we're that old. It's ..." Iris stopped abruptly and turned back to her desk. I saw her fingers grip the cover of a book.

"Yes, I know. I know." I slid off the bed. I couldn't bear to think about it. I couldn't stand to think about losing Gran and Grandad. It still hurt so much to think about losing my mum.

"It's different from Mum," said Iris. I guessed she was thinking the same thing. Her voice was muffled, and she stared down at her book. "It's natural to die when you're old."

There was a long silence. I wasn't thinking anything. My mind was all jumbled and tangled. Then Iris said, "Keep busy, Rose. That's what I do." She straightened the books neatly on her desk. "It will stop you worrying."

I didn't see that. I didn't see how you could stop worrying. But I didn't say anything more.

I went to the bathroom and locked the door. It's the only place in the house that's private.

I felt the scream rising into my throat, so I did what I used to do after Mum died. I turned the faucets on full, until the room was full of steam, and then I opened the cupboard door and drove my fists into the piles of towels like they were punching bags. I hit them and hit them and hit them until my arms ached — and all the time I cried and cried. I punched and cried until I had no more tears left inside me, and my stomach hurt.

And it wasn't until much later that I remembered I hadn't asked Iris about Dad selling our house.

7

The Repo Men

THE NEXT MORNING, after the "great kidnapping caper," as Basil called it, things were almost calm around our house. Dad didn't say anything about Gran going away, and so I decided maybe he'd forgotten about it. I really wanted to talk to Dad about Gran, but I was worried that if I did it might remind him about the nursing home, so I said nothing.

I had decided that if I tried really hard I could watch Gran carefully and stop anything bad from happening. When school was over, I hurried home even faster than usual.

A red tow truck was parked outside our house. I could see two men hitching a tow bar onto the back bumper of our truck. This surprised me. Dad always did all the repairs himself. We had no money to send it to the garage.

"Hi!" I said to the men. "What garage is our truck going to?"

One of the men, who had long ginger hair tied back in a ponytail, laughed at me. "No garage, kid," he said, and he hit at the tow bar with a mallet.

"Shut up, stupid," said the other man. He was very fat, with tattoos all over his arms. I stared at the tattoos. Twisted blue snakes with great fangs coiled round red hearts.

"Don't call me stupid," said the man with the ponytail. "Kid asks a question, I tell her the truth."

"Where are you taking our truck then?" I asked quickly. I don't know why, but I had a sudden feeling that something was wrong.

"We're the repo men," he said. "Yep. We're the friendly neighbourhood repo men."

"Repo men?" I didn't know what he meant, but it sounded bad.

The fat man with the tattoos climbed into the cab of the tow truck and gunned the motor.

"Tighten up that bar and let's get out of here, Steve," he yelled.

"Does my Dad know you're taking our truck?" I shouted. And I ran forward and stood right in front of the tow truck with my arms stuck out. "Dad! Dad!" I shouted as loud as I could. "Dad, come quick!"

"Get out of the way, kid!" The fat man stuck his head out the window. "We're only doing our job."

What did he mean? What was his job? "Dad! Dad!" My voice cracked with my screaming.

But it was Basil who came running first. He must have been coming around the corner because he galloped up to me in great long strides.

"Rose, what's the matter?" He was puffing, out of breath.

"They're taking our truck," I pointed at the two men. "They say they're repo men — whatever that is!"

"Oh no!" Basil glared at the men. "Don't move. I'll get Dad."

It seemed a long, long time before Dad came racing down the steps of our house, but I suppose it was only a minute. I was scared, but I didn't move. I didn't really think the fat man would drive over me, but he kept shouting for me to get out of the way, honking the horn and revving up the tow-truck engine.

Dad's face was beet red. "If you take the truck I can't get any work," he told the two men, and he banged hard on the tow-truck door with the side of his hand. "If I can't get work, your company will never get paid."

Basil and I stood on the steps and waited and waited while Dad tried to persuade the men not to drive away with our truck.

"How can these guys just come and take it?" I asked Basil. "Isn't it stealing?"

"They can take the truck because we owe money," Basil said. "*Repo* is short for *repossession*. Repo men are hired by collection agencies to take back stuff that people can't pay for — like cars and trucks."

"Dad's right," I said. "If those guys take our

Green Thumb truck, he won't be able to work."

"I know," said Basil.

I tried not to think. If Dad couldn't work we wouldn't have any money at all!

Then Goldy arrived home from school, and I had to explain to her what repo men were, and how I had stood in front of the truck to stop the men from taking it.

"Oh, Rose, that's scary! You were brave," she said.

I didn't say anything, but I guess I was, a bit.

Finally the two men and Dad shook hands, and the guy with the ponytail unhooked the tow bar.

We all cheered.

"Five days." Dad hurried up the steps to where we were standing. "They've let us have five more days to come up with the money." Just five days! I thought. That was Saturday; hardly any time at all. But I didn't say anything out loud. Everyone looked so worried, I didn't dare.

8

The Mysterious Box

AFTER THE REPO men left, I wandered into the kitchen. It was a good thing Gran hadn't seen them. She'd have been very upset. As it was, she seemed just fine. She stood at the kitchen sink peeling potatoes, and there was a rich smell of peanut butter cookies in the air.

"How are you feeling?" I asked her.

"Not so tired today, Rose, thank goodness. Heaven knows why I got so exhausted yesterday. I must have cleaned the house in my sleep."

I chewed a cookie and didn't say anything. Gran didn't remember a thing about running away or searching for a box. Grandad told me not to mention it. Today she was having a GD and it would only worry her if we told her what she'd done yesterday. Grandad said that if Gran got worried on her GDs then they might stop being GDs altogether. It made perfect sense to me.

But Gran had noticed some strange things in the kitchen. "Someone's emptied all the spice boxes!" she complained at dinner. "Why would anyone empty spice boxes?" She looked around the table. "Was it you, Goldy? Are you doing a project at school that you need little boxes for?"

I held my breath. It must have been Gran who emptied the spices, when she was searching for her lost box.

"It wasn't me, Gran!" Goldy shot a look at Dad. Dad stopped shaking salt on his potatoes and shook his head instead. Goldy was disappointed, but she shut up. I bet she had a hard time keeping quiet. Her face looked as if it would burst. Goldy loved to talk.

There was a sudden choking sound, and Dad started to cough and go red in the face.

"Dad!" Basil reached over and banged him on the back.

"Sugar!" Dad screwed up his face. "Sugar! Ugh!"

"What?" Basil banged him harder.

"Sugar in the salt shaker!" Dad wiped his face with a napkin. "Ugh!"

"Now, I wonder how that happened," Gran said in a puzzled voice. "Do you think the salt company made a mistake?"

No one said anything. But I guessed we were all thinking the same thing.

"Oh well." Dad took a big gulp of water. "Look on the bright side. At least it wasn't strychnine."

Iris looked up. "Strychnine! Why do you want strychnine?"

"No, Iris," said Grandad. "There is no strychnine. Your father is just making a joke."

"Strychnine is no joke." Iris wrinkled her forehead. "It's a deadly poison."

"Iris!" Dad closed his eyes and groaned. "If you can't listen to the conversation, just be quiet."

Then he opened his eyes and stared at her. Dad also had a complaint. "And speaking of quiet, what were you doing this morning, girl?" he said irritably. "Were you walking around with army boots on?"

Iris has to get up very early to take the bus to college. She makes a lot of noise around the house and wakes up everyone, except me, when she bangs the cupboard doors and turns on taps. She doesn't mean to wake everyone. She just doesn't notice that she's noisy. She doesn't wake me because I'm always awake and wandering around as soon as it gets light. But Dad wakes up if the foghorn hoots in the bay or if rain patters on the roof. He sometimes wakes in the middle of the night and doesn't know what he heard, and that drives him wild and he wanders around the house, up and down the stairs, looking for the phantom noise. However, when Dad hears sounds in the early morning, he certainly knows it's Iris.

"Oh, Dad." Iris just smiled at him. Her thoughts were obviously far away, with some exciting bacteria or chemical formula I guessed. Iris never seemed to notice that what she did affected anybody, but no one really got cross with her either. She was just Iris. Dad has given up trying to get her to help around the house.

It wouldn't be fair to say that she isn't cooperative. She is. "Sure," she says when Dad asks her to pick up groceries or wash clothes. And she smiles. "Of course," she says. But then she instantly forgets. And we have no milk and no clean underwear! Anyway, except for the repo men, the spice boxes and Iris's noise, things were really calm — until Tuesday.

When I got home from school on Tuesday, I could see Gran in the garden. She was standing by the rose bed with a spade.

"Gran, what are you doing?" I ran along the path towards her. Gran is not a gardener like Dad and Grandad. "Goodness knows why I married a gardener," she sometimes teased Grandad. "All that dirt tracked into the house."

Now Gran stared at me. "Josephine! What a surprise. Lovely to see you." She settled her straw hat firmly on her curls.

"Cessy," I said. "What are you doing?"

"Looking for my box," she said, and she stared around at the roses.

"I'm sure my box is out here." Gran shook her head. "My box is full of roses."

"Have I seen this box?" Gran had a whole shelf of ornaments in her sitting room. Maybe I knew what it looked like.

"Of course, Josephine." She smiled, as though I'd asked her a silly question. "Don't you remember? You gave it to me."

"I did?" I said. I was getting muddled up with being me and Great Aunt Josephine, both at the same time.

"Of course you did." Gran looked at the roses again. "I'm having trouble digging, Josephine," she said sadly. "Will you dig up the roses for me? I must find my box. My box will save us. And I know it's under the roses."

I blinked. Dig up Grandad's prize roses! I didn't know what to say.

"Please help me, Josephine." Gran touched me on the arm and gave me a pleading look. "I must find my box. I must find my box."

"Couldn't we dig somewhere else. Gran ... er, Cessy," I said, staring around the garden, looking for a better place.

Our garden is a muddle of tame and wild. The wild parts are Dad's. He likes mossy grass, overhanging shrubs and volunteers like foxgloves and yarrow. I think he likes this kind of garden because my mother did. The tame part is Grandad's. He likes ordered rows of vegetables, neat clipped hedges and weeded borders of pansies and staked dahlias. I think that both my dad and my grandad look a lot like the garden. Dad looks rather wild. His beard is all straggly and he forgets to get his hair cut. He hates dressing up, and his clothes look rumpled and creased. Grandad, however, is always tidy. His hair is cut so short it feels like a stubby brush. He always wears a tie and an ironed shirt, and he polishes his shoes so you can see your face in the sheen.

I ran over to the rows of dark green cabbages. "Why don't we dig here," I said. I didn't like cabbage, so I didn't mind digging up a few of those.

"But, Josephine," Gran shook her head, "my box is here." She pointed to the roses. "I need my box. The roses ..."

Well, what could I do? I took the spade, looked towards the house to see if Grandad was watching, and started to dig.

I started with the weakest rose bush — Yellow Blush, its called. It had mildewed leaves and quite a lot of black spots, so I didn't feel too bad about uprooting it. It took me a while, but I finally got it up.

"There's nothing there, Cessy." I showed her the hole. "No box." I was hoping that one bush would be enough to convince her. Dig another one, Josephine." Gran pointed at a Peace rose with large yellow blooms.

I dug up the Peace, an Old Fashioned, a Crimson Fire and a Red Ruby. Of course, none of them had a box underneath.

And then Gran pointed to the one bush I'd been hoping she'd ignore. "Try that one, Josephine," she said, pointing at Grandad's pride and joy, a rose bush with tiny mauve blooms and a mauvy smell to match. *The Lady Cecilia*, Grandad's very own creation. He named the rose in honour of Gran, and it had won a gold medal at a competition.

"Yes," said Gran. "My box is under that bush. I know it is."

I could feel my face get all red and hot and prickly drops of sweat dripped down my arms and legs. I kept looking from the coloured petals strewn across the earth to the house — and wishing that Grandad would come outside and stop me.

And then he did. He came out of the French doors onto the patio. He was yawning. I guess he'd been having his afternoon nap.

"Oh!" he said as he saw the piles of earth and the rose bushes lying with their roots in the air. "What's happened? Rose, did you dig up my roses?" His voice sounded shocked. "Did you dig up *The Lady Cecilia*?"

"Yes," I said, "but Gran asked me to," I added quickly. I knew he would never get cross with Gran.

"Oh," he said again. And I was right; he said it very gently. "Cessy?"

"I'm looking for my box." Gran frowned. It's got roses in it. My box will save us. I must find my box. I must. I must."

"Mmm!" Grandad took Granny's arm and led her inside. "Rose will make you a cup of tea."

"Sure," I said. I could tell from Grandad's tone that he didn't believe in Gran's box. I didn't myself. I mean, who would bury a box under some rose bushes?

So, I sat down with Gran and drank tea while Grandad replanted all the roses.

9

Food Hunt!

GRAN MUST HAVE spent all day looking for her box. At least, that's what I figured out later, after Dad came back from the supermarket.

Dad had the week's groceries.

"Ten bags!" I counted as I helped him pack all the stuff away.

"A record," said Dad, but he didn't smile. I guess he was worried about how much the food cost.

"You didn't get any cans of tuna, Dad." I looked through the bags. "We don't have any left."

"What? But I bought a big box last week at the discount store."

"Well, there's none left now. Basil was trying

to make tuna-fish sandwiches, and he couldn't find any."

"How can one family eat forty-four cans of tuna in seven days!" Dad started to rummage through the cupboards. "It's impossible!"

"And you didn't buy any sugar," I told him. "We're out of sugar too."

"I bought two giant bags last week!" Dad's voice began to rise. "We can't have used fifty pounds of sugar! That has to last us for months."

I shrugged. I decided I'd better not mention we were out of toilet paper as well.

"Dad, did you get toothpaste?" Basil came into the kitchen, holding his toothbrush.

"Toothpaste!" Dad's voice gave a sort of squeak. "I bought one of those economy boxes. It must be in the bathroom somewhere!"

"I can't find any," said Basil.

"I don't understand!" Dad moved to the freezer with an armload of bread. "Where's all this stuff got to?"

Then he gave a little scream and dropped the bread on the floor.

"Toilet paper!" he yelped.

Basil and I ran over to look. The whole freezer was full of toilet paper. Dozens of rolls.

"Where's all the frozen food gone?" Basil started rummaging through the toilet paper rolls. "There should be at least twenty bags of frozen blackberries."

"I'll say," I said. "I can still feel all those scratches I got when we went picking last September."

"I seem to remember that you ate everything you picked," said Basil, and he ruffled my hair.

I picked up a roll of toilet paper and threw it at him.

He ducked and the paper hit Dad.

"Stop it, Rosy." Dad started rubbing his beard so hard I thought it might come off. "Where are all the frozen peas, and that salmon I was given?"

I found all the frozen food myself. I carried the frozen toilet paper down to the basement storeroom, and I saw a great mass of red juice puddling across the floor from a cupboard. The blackberries!

"Hmm," was all Dad said. He knew it must be Gran who moved everything. "I guess she was looking for her box and moved things around," I said, as we wiped up the mess.

"I guess so," was all he said back. Basil found the tuna in the cupboard under the stairs, and I found the sugar in the broom closet, but we didn't find the toothpaste.

"I think we should secrete the cereal," Basil said to me.

"Don't use big words," I said, throwing punches at him.

"Come on!" Basil started feinting at the air around me. "Hit me as hard as you can!"

So I did. I danced around him, punching and jabbing until my arms were tired. Hitting Basil is like hitting a concrete wall. He just laughed. He didn't feel a thing.

"Now. Let's conceal the cereal." Basil grinned at me. "It would be a calamity if Gran hides that and we can't find it."

I made a face at him, then I figured he meant that it would be a disaster if there was no cereal at breakfast. I agreed with that! So we hid the Cheerios and cornflakes carefully behind the kitchen radiator.

***

Later that evening I was lying on the couch, watching a game show on TV, and trying to juggle three tennis balls. I had the idea that if I could get to be a great juggler, I could juggle outside the Granville market and people would throw loonies into a hat. That way I'd get some allowance. It wasn't easy. I kept dropping the balls, and they kept rolling and bouncing all over the room.

And then — POW! Goldy sat down on top of me.

"Oof!" I shouted. The tennis balls skittered in all directions. "Get off! What did you have to do that for?" And I kicked out at her.

"Go away!" She screamed and grabbed the remote control from under me.

"I'll tell Dad." She zapped off the game show.

"So tell!" I grabbed the remote back from her and zapped the game show back again. "I had this first."

"Rose, guess what?" Goldy's voice suddenly changed. "Guess what Gran's doing now?"

"What?"

"She's taken all the books out of the bookcase and put them in piles on the floor. What is she looking for, Rose?" Goldy spoke as if I should know the answer.

"Her box," I said. "You know that."

"But there isn't a box." Goldy pulled a face. "Gran's just making it up. How could a box be under a bunch of old roses?"

"I don't know." I rolled onto the floor and scrabbled for my balls. "Gran can't help it if her memory is all wrong."

"But why is her memory all wrong?"

"I don't know," I said. I wished Goldy wouldn't ask me questions like that. "Nobody knows. Maybe because she's worried."

"But if you lost all your memory, you wouldn't be worried, would you?" asked Goldy.

80

"Gran's not losing all her memory." I got two balls into the air. Maybe I should stick with two. "She remembers her sister."

"And things she did when she was a kid," Goldy said slowly. "Isn't that strange?"

"It's like her memory is a hard drive with lots of wiped-out bits," I said. "Like you deleted my speech for that social studies project."

Goldy flicked the channels with the remote control. "And when she gets to a wiped-out bit, she doesn't even know it's wiped out." She flicked the channels faster. "And I told you I didn't mean to erase that socials stuff. It was an accident."

"Hmm," I said. "It's not always the same stuff on the hard drive that Gran forgets. It's more like it's the computer that doesn't work properly."

I liked that thought. I liked the idea of Gran's memories being pictures and music on a hard drive that were all mixed up by a weird computer.

"My friend Cathy thinks that Gran is going mad."

I hurled both the balls into the corner of the room. "What does that stupid Cathy know?" I

81

said. "She can't even run. She waddles like a duck."

I left the TV to Goldy and went to look for Gran. I found her in the hallway crouched down by the hall cupboard, pulling out umbrellas.

"Gran! What are you doing?"

"Ah, Josephine." Gran held up a broken black umbrella. "Put this on the dining room table for me." She straightened up with a little groan, her hand on her back. "Be careful. My box may be inside it."

I took the umbrella and did as Gran said. And then I watched as she got the rest of the umbrellas from the cupboard and laid them in a line on the dining room table. Besides the black one with the broken spine, there was a yellow umbrella with pink dots, a golf umbrella with red and green stripes and Goldy's baby umbrella, blue with white kittens chasing each other around the edge.

"Really, Mum." Dad followed us into the dining room, with a scouring pad in his hand, and watched Gran look carefully inside each umbrella.

"How could a box be inside an umbrella?" He spoke slowly. "Think about it. It just doesn't make sense." He was already upset because Gran had forgotten she'd put the vegetables on the stove, and they had boiled dry and burnt the saucepan. It was too bad because the vegetables were Grandad's new peas and carrots from the garden.

"My box is here somewhere." Gran shook the golf umbrella, almost stabbing Dad with the point.

Dad jumped backwards to safety. "In the umbrella?" He sighed. "You're not being logical, Mum."

"It is here. It is," said Gran tearfully. "I need it. It will save us …" But then she left the umbrellas, wandered into the living room and started picking up the cushions from the chairs. "Blue velvet," she said, holding onto a blue velvet cushion. "It's blue velvet!"

"Your box is blue velvet?" Dad gave her a funny look. I could see he thought Gran was totally out of it. "Is that it?"

Gran cradled the cushion in her arms. "I don't know who you are." She stared at him.

"I'm Brian." Dad threw his arms out wide. "I'm your son."

It was no good. Gran didn't recognize him. I just can't see why Dad gets so upset.

When I was getting ready for bed, I found the blue velvet cushion on the kitchen table. It was cut open, and the stuffing was falling out. I couldn't think why Gran wanted to cut it up. Did she really think her box was inside the blue velvet cushion? Nobody else noticed, so I put all the bits in a plastic bag and hid it on the top shelf of the hall closet.

All the next day in school I sat and tried to think of ways to keep Gran safe. But I kept returning to the same old idea — I had to try to watch her as much as I could. Every time I even thought of my gran being sent away to some nursing home, I felt sick. I couldn't bear the thought of her being sent away. And, as soon as school was over, I raced for home.

"Wait up, Rose!" Goldy yelled behind me.

"You're supposed to wait for me. I'll tell on you."

"So, tell!" I yelled back. But I didn't stop. It's all uphill to our house from the school, And I can see the roof from five blocks away. There's green moss growing all over the shakes and the chimney leans to one side. Mum used to say our house was a character house. I would agree with that. Our house's character is pretty untidy, and it needs a face lift. The yellow paint on the shingles is mostly worn off and the front steps, which used to be painted black, are now bald and slope to the right. The kitchen slopes to the left, and the bathroom on the main floor seems to slope in every direction. I know this because I have tried putting a marble down in each of these places and watching which direction it rolls. The only part of our house that isn't character is the bit in the basement that Dad built for Gran and Grandad. He took my bedroom and turned it into a bathroom for them, and the old rec room is now their living room (so they can escape from us) with glass doors that open onto a patio in the backyard.

As soon as I turned the corner of our block, I

could see something was happening outside our house. Mrs. Dunk, Pepi and a whole lot of neighbours were standing on the sidewalk. And there was a police car! Police! I ran faster. My breath came in great gasps. "Gran," I said over and over. "Gran!"

10

Burglars!

THERE WERE TWO policemen inside the house — the same policemen who had come before. The ones Goldy said were called Jesse and James. They were in Gran and Grandad's living room in the basement.

"What happened?" I burst into the room. "Is Gran hurt?"

"No." Grandad smiled at me. "It's all right, Rose. Your grandmother called the police." He had on his tweed gardening hat and his rubber-boots, and he was holding a trowel in his hands.

"A burglar has been here, Josephine." Gran nodded at me from the couch, where she was tucked up with a tartan rug over her knees. "I called the police!"

"What's been stolen?" I stared around the room. Maybe it was the TV and the VCR from upstairs. We don't have anything else that's worth taking. One of the two policemen, Jesse, I think, cleared his throat. He was the tall one, who swayed. His head was so close to the ceiling that his cap brushed the plaster.

"Mrs. Green says that a very valuable box has been stolen." He looked at me steadily. "Do you know anything about this box?"

"Oh!" I didn't know what to say. I snuck a glance at Grandad, but he was humming a little tune and looking out at the patio. "Well," I said, "Gran has been looking for a box ..."

"Mrs. Green doesn't seem to be able to describe this box." The short policeman, James, spoke slowly. "She says a box has been stolen, but she doesn't know what it looks like."

"Oh!" I said again. It was all I could think of.

"Officer, please will you start to search for the burglar?" Gran started to get up from the couch. Her hair was all mussed up, and she looked like a wild bird. "I must have my box back. I must ... I must. My box can save us."

"Shhh! Cessy," Grandad went over and patted her hand. "It's all right. The officers will do what they can."

"Of course," said Jesse. He looked down at James, and James looked up at him. I could tell they thought that Gran was just making it all up about the box. But they were very nice. They didn't say so.

"I'll see you out," said Grandad, and they went upstairs.

I looked carefully around the room. Had there really been a burglar? Gran had such a clutter of things in the room I wasn't sure I would notice anything missing. Besides a worn flowered sofa and two armchairs, there was an old red persian carpet, a round oak coffee table, an oil painting of a peasant girl with cherries in a basket, seven plaster geese in different sizes from tiny to large flying in a V across one wall, a set of round china plates showing pictures of baby animals on another wall, a glass-fronted china cabinet with two pink conch shells on top and a set of best china with red roses inside, a bookcase full of faded red-and-green photo albums, two ivory-coloured floor lamps, a window sill full of plants, a telephone covered with a crocheted crinoline doll, a calendar displaying the country of the month, which was Holland, a clock with a glass cover and a soft ticking pendulum, a stool with daisies embroidered on the seat — and that was just for starters. There was a whole shelf of photographs as well, but no box that I could see.

I picked up a photograph in a silver frame and stared at it. It was an old, faded photo of Great Aunt Josephine. Her wedding picture. Great Aunt Josephine stared back at me from the past. She had a jewelled tiara in her hair and diamond earrings like shimmering, glittering stars, dangling from her ears.

"Josephine always dripped with jewels," Gran had told me. I liked that expression. I'd like to meet someone who "dripped with jewels." I wished I had met Great Aunt Josephine. I put the photo carefully back on the shelf.

"Did you see the burglar?" I asked Gran.

"I went to have my afternoon rest." Gran twisted a fringe on the blanket around her fingers. "And when I came back out here I just knew there had been someone here. My box was gone, you see."

"Oh, Gran ... Cessy."

"Oh, it's all right, Josephine," she said in a tiny voice. "You never believe me."

"Oh, yes I do." I rushed over and gave her a hug. "I'm sorry. If you say your box has been stolen, I believe you." I couldn't bear to see her looking so hurt. If my Gran wanted to have a hundred burglars, it was fine with me. I didn't really believe her, but so what?

Gran put her thin brown arm around my shoulders. "I'm sure the burglar will come back. I want to set a trap for him," she said. "Will you help me?"

"A trap?" I was a bit doubtful about this. "What sort of trap?"

"A flour trap, I think." Gran spoke slowly, as though she was reaching far back into the past. "We used to make flour traps when we were chil-

dren, do you remember? They were very successful." She smiled a memory smile.

"You used to make traps when you were a little girl?" I could hardly believe it.

"Mm, yes, well so did you. Don't you remember?"

"Not really," I told her truthfully. I'd never
thought of making a trap in my life, but now I felt
quite excited and couldn't see why I hadn't. "How
do we do it?"

"Well," Gran sat up straight, "I've been thinking. I think we'll put a trap over that door," and
she pointed to the patio door. "That's the only
way anyone could sneak inside. We have it open
for fresh air."

"All right," I said.

So we did. Under Gran's directions, I brought
down a bag of white flour from the kitchen, stood
on a chair and balanced the bag on the frame
above the door. Then she had me get a long piece
of string. The string was tied to the door handle
and then pulled up the length of the door and
across the top. The other end of the string was

tied around the open bag of flour. If anyone pushed the door open the string would tighten and down would come the whole sack of flour — right on top of them.

"It's so simple, but so clever!" I said admiringly.

Gran clapped her hands. "Oh, how this takes me back. Do you remember when we set a trap for Henry, that big bully who came visiting with his mother?" She clapped her hands again and giggled. "What a mess. He was so mad, and so was Mother. Remember we had to go to bed without any supper!"

"Well, no, I don't remember," I said. Of course I didn't, but I was very sorry I hadn't been there and seen Henry the bully getting trapped.

"Well, you two look like the cat who's swallowed the cream," said Grandad as he came into the room and pulled on his old plaid slippers. "What are you up to?"

"Never you mind," said Gran. "Josephine and I have a little secret."

"Still Josephine, is it?" said Grandad and he

gave me a look that meant, "Is everything all right?" And I smiled back at him to show it was.

***

Now, I didn't believe in Gran's burglar, of course, but I did want to see someone get trapped and floured and I spent the rest of the evening wondering what excuse I could use to get Basil or Goldy onto the deck, down the stairs, and back into the house through the patio doors.

"Do you hear a strange noise?" I asked Basil, as we loaded the dishwasher after dinner. "I think it's coming from Gran and Grandad's patio!"

He listened. "I don't hear anything. Probably some old cat on the prowl. Can you finish now, Rose? I've got to get back to school for basketball practice."

"I keep hearing a strange noise down on the patio," I said to Goldy, who was hunched in front of the TV. I was sure she'd jump at this. Goldy makes a story out of everything.

"Shhh!" she hissed at me, her eyes fixed on the

screen. "It's *Operation X* and Mandy doesn't know there's someone in the closet. He's got an axe!"

"Goldy, turn that off!" Dad came into the room with three of Grandad's ties on his arm. "You'll have a nightmare."

"Oh! Dad! It's Rose who has nightmares, not me!" Goldy moved closer to the TV. "She's the one who has to have a night light!"

"Dad!" I felt my face going red. "She's not supposed to bug me!" It's true I had a night light — I hated to wake up in the dark — but Goldy wasn't supposed to tease me about it.

"Marigold!"

"Oh, it's not fair!" Goldy nicked the remote control and threw it on the floor. "Other kids don't have to keep turning off the TV everytime there's a decent program. I never get to watch anything. You treat me like a baby." She threw a cushion after the remote. "I hate you all!"

"I know," said Dad. "Don't tell me. You're going to run away and make us sorry. Right?"

"Yes, I am!" shouted Goldy. "I really am this time!" She flounced out of the room and slammed the door behind her.

I didn't get too upset about this. Goldy was always threatening to run away, but she never did.

"That girl!" Dad flung himself down on the sofa. Dad always said this too.

"Help me choose a tie," he said, laying the three ties over his knee. "Which one will impress the credit union manager?"

"This one." I held up a blue-and-red striped tie. "It looks very serious."

"Good," said Dad. "That's the one then."

"Dad!" I said, remembering the trap. "You know, I keep hearing strange noises down on the patio."

"Really, Rosy." He ruffled my hair. "Don't you start hearing things. You're the only sensible person around here. It's bad enough with your grandmother seeing things all over the place and going loopy-loop! Burglars! I'll probably get a bill from the police for wasting their time!"

"Dad!" I pummelled him on the chest, hard, with both my fists. "Gran's not loopy-loop. What a mean thing to say."

"Ouch!" Dad caught hold of my arms. "Rosy, listen. I'm sorry. It was just a joke. You know I didn't mean it."

"I love Gran. I don't mind if she thinks I'm Great Aunt Josephine. I don't mind if she forgets who I am. She's still my gran."

"I know," said Dad. "I'm the one who gets upset. I love her too." He sighed. "Sometimes when things are hard to deal with we have to make little jokes and laugh. It makes us feel better. But it doesn't mean we don't care."

I sniffed.

"That's right." Dad wiped my eyes with a tissue. "Come on. Let's have a smile," and he moved my lips upwards into a smile with two fingers.

So I had to laugh at that and then we hugged each other and I felt better, until I got woken up in the middle of the night — and then I must admit I felt very guilty.

11

Burglars Again!

AT FIRST I thought I was having a bad dream, and I lay with my eyes staring open, and my heart pounding in my ears. But then I realized it was a real police siren outside our house that woke me. It's hard to sleep through a police siren, especially when your room is at the front and the red light from the police car flashes round and round the walls.

There was a sharp sudden silence as the wailing was abruptly cut off and then a great deal of noise came up from the basement. Shouting and banging and crashing. I got out of bed and ran to see what was happening.

When everything was sorted out later, I figured this was what I had missed:

1. Dad woke up in the middle of the night and heard a noise.

2. He remembered what I said about noises on the patio and decided to investigate.

3. Dad crept out of the kitchen onto the deck and down the stairs to the patio. He saw the door was ajar and pushed it open.

4. Down came the sack of flour on top of Dad.

5. Dad shouted and staggered around, banging into furniture and knocking plants and ornaments onto the floor.

6. Gran heard the noise and got up to see what was happening. Grandad had his hearing aid turned off and kept sleeping.

7. Gran saw what she thought was a burglar, covered in flour, and phoned the police.

8. Dad tried to reason with Gran, but Gran was having a BD. She didn't rec-

ognize him and gave him a lecture about stealing her box.

9. The police arrived.

10. I woke up.

I couldn't believe it! Jesse and James were at our house again! I don't think they could believe it either.

"Who do you think I am then?" Dad shouted at them. "Do I look like a burglar? Don't you recognize me? You were talking to me three days ago." As he shouted and waved his arms around, great streamers of white flour clouded the air. Dad was covered in flour. The trap was one hundred percent successful! If it wasn't for his voice and his funny rubber slippers, I wouldn't know Dad myself. His face was like a clown's and his hair stuck up in great white spikes around his bald spot.

"Well, sir, it's rather difficult to see who you are at present," said Constable Jesse, looking down at my father.

"We have a complaint about intruders and we are obliged to investigate," said Constable James in a formal voice, looking up, but he shot a sideways glance at Gran who was standing next to him. In her baby blue dressing gown, with her white hair curling around her face, my gran seemed like the most innocent person in the world.

"You see," Gran smiled at the policemen, "I was right. I said there was a burglar. Will you get him to give me my box? Everything will be all right when I get my box."

"Mother! For heaven's sake!" Dad wailed, sending more flour into the air. "I'm Brian, your son!"

"Nonsense!" Gran frowned at him. "My son, Brian, is a young man with a full head of hair. Josephine knows we are trapping a burglar."

"That's not Josephine. That's Rosy." Dad hit the side of his head with his hand. At that moment everyone else arrived, and things got more muddled. Grandad, who was still half asleep and hadn't turned on his hearing aid, thought that Gran had run away again and been brought back by the police.

"Thank you. Thank you." He shook their hands and thanked them over and over. I think this sort of confused Constable Jesse and Constable James.

"Is it a fire? Is it a fire?" Goldy rubbed her eyes and kept sniffing for smoke. Basil kept saying, "What's going on then? What's going on then?" in a slow, sleep-walking tone of voice. As for Iris, she just threw herself into a chair, where she sat with her hair hanging to her waist, and yawned and yawned.

"Who is this man?" Officer Jesse pointed at flour-covered Dad.

"Dad!" said Goldy.

"Father!" said Basil.

"My son!" said Grandad.

"A burglar!" cried Gran.

"But, Dad, why are you covered in white stuff?" Goldy said in a puzzled voice.

"It's not Hallowe'en, is it?" Iris said, surprised.

"What's going on?" said Basil, for the tenth time.

"It's my son, officer." Grandad spoke as if he were introducing Dad. "However, he's not generally covered in flour."

After all this, Officer Jesse and Officer James gave us all a warning about phoning the police without due cause. Then they gave Dad a very odd look, shook Grandad by the hand once more, as he thanked them once again for bringing Gran safely home, and left. I think they would have liked to book Dad for something, but they couldn't think of an offence. I guess there is no law against people walking around their own houses covered in flour. And they couldn't book Gran. She really did think Dad was a burglar.

"Well," said Grandad, rubbing his hands. "I vote we all go back to bed. All's well that ends well."

"How can you say that?" Dad's voice rose. "Here am I covered in flour. The police think I'm crazy. My own mother doesn't know me and thinks I'm a burglar." He brushed white flour into spirals across the floor. "And who set this idiotic trap anyway?" He glared around the room.

"What do you mean, Brian? Of course I know you." Gran pointed a finger at him. "What are you talking about?" With that, she walked towards the bedroom door. "What I don't understand is why you're covered in flour in the middle of the night and why we're all standing around listening to you. Arthur is right. We should go to bed." She stopped. "Look at the poor children. They're exhausted." She blew us all a kiss and closed the door.

"Well!" Dad spluttered. "Of all the ..." He could hardly speak.

I hugged myself. Oh, my gran! What great timing. I could hardly stop from laughing.

"Marvellous!" said Grandad. "Gran is back in GD form. She knows who you are, Brian."

"Hmmp!" said Dad.

***

Of course after this the whole twisted story came out, and I had to own up to helping Gran with the trap.

"Gran thought she'd catch a burglar, Dad," I tried to explain. "She thought a burglar stole her box." I didn't think I needed to tell him that I also wanted to see if the trap worked. I couldn't help feeling guilty about trapping Dad, but mostly I felt excited that the trap had worked so well.

"For goodness sake, Rosy." Dad pulled at his beard. "If your grandmother starts doing crazy things, don't aid and abet her. Come and tell me. This isn't a game."

12

Emergency!

I WAS THE one who saw the fire first, even if Goldy did tell everybody it was her.

Gran met me as I arrived home from school on Thursday afternoon and hustled me across the lawn to the cedar tree at the end of the garden.

"I want you to climb the cedar, Josephine."

Gran pointed upwards. "I really think my box may be up there. Yes." She nodded firmly. "In the cedar tree."

We stood side by side under the drooping green branches. "But, Gran," I said. "I mean, Cessy ... " I choked over the words. My throat was tight, and I could feel my legs starting to tremble. The cedar was in my dream almost every night, but I hadn't climbed it since Mum died. "I can't!" I said finally.

"But, Josephine," Gran shook her head, "you love climbing trees. Don't you remember the maple tree in our backyard? Don't you remember how you got smacked for climbing the tree and tearing your best petticoat?"

"No," I said. I didn't know what else to say, and I scuffed my shoes into the cedar bits around the trunk.

Gran looked at me and her face crumpled inwards as if I'd hit her.

"All right. All right!" I put my books down on the grass. I couldn't bear to see Gran look so upset. I'd do anything to stop her looking like that — even climb the cedar. I took a deep breath of cedar smell, grabbed hold of the lowest branch and swung myself upwards.

It was an easy tree to climb. The branches were like steps, but I started to shake like a leaf as soon as I reached the first one, and I had to grab hold of the trunk to stop from falling. It took ages to edge myself up to the next branch, and when I got there I stopped.

"Nothing here," I said, pretending to look all around and hoping that Gran would give up.

"Go higher," Gran ordered. "Maybe my box is higher."

So I inched slowly upwards to the next branch. It was the branch that was in my dream — a thick branch, rubbed smooth from sitting — the branch where I counted the freighters.

My dream came from a real memory. When I was little, before I went to school, that's what I used to do, sit on the branch in the sunshine and count freighters while Mum gardened. It was how I learned to count.

"Is my box there, Josephine?" Gran's voice drifted up to me. "Can you see my box?"

"No," I called back. "There's no box here." Of course there wasn't. Gran was crazy to think there might be.

My fingers and toes had begun to tremble, as if it was winter and I was freezing cold. I wanted to climb down, but I was shaking so much I was scared I'd slip and fall.

I sat on the branch, gripped onto the trunk, and stared out over English Bay. There were the freighters waiting to load up with grain, all pulling at their anchors, their bows pointing out to sea. The tide was going out. I started to count them without even thinking. Four rusty orange ones flying the green-and-white flag of Panama, two shiny black ones with the red-sun flag of Japan, one grey battleship from China, and five more — anchored too far on the other side for me to see where they were from. Twelve. It wasn't like my dream. I didn't have to count twice. Twelve. No doubt about it.

I leaned my head back against the splintery trunk and felt the sun warm against my face, and suddenly it wasn't so bad. My hands and feet stopped shaking. And I was glad I'd climbed the tree. It was like being back with a friend.

"Josephine!" Gran called out again. "Can you see my box?"

Poor Gran. She really was upset, and I wished I could make magic and find a box for her hidden in the tree. "Here it is!" I'd say, and I'd carry it down and place it in her hands.

"Sorry, Cessy ..." I began to say, when clouds of black smoke started pouring out of the kitchen window.

"There's a fire!" I gave a sort of squeaking call. And then I heard Goldy yelling, "Fire! Fire! Call Emergency!"

I was in such a rush to get to the fire, that I was hardly aware of climbing down. I just remember sliding over the last bit fast and banging my knee.

I'd never seen so much black smoke. The kitchen was full of it. Dense black clouds poured out of the oven in great billowing waves. I waved my hands in front of my face, and started to cough. The smoke caught at the back of my throat and tickled and burned.

"Get out of here, Rose!" Grandad came into the room, puffing and blowing, like he had climbed the stairs fast. He put a tea towel across his face and crossed the room and switched off the oven.

We hurried outside. I coughed and coughed and Goldy banged me on the back.

"Too bad there weren't any flames," said Goldy.

"I wanted to call the fire department. But Grandad wouldn't let me."

Even if there weren't any flames, the smoke sure made a mess. It turned out the fire had started because Gran left the oven on broil to brown a casserole, then went out into the garden to look for her box, and forgot about it. The casserole started to burn and smoke poured out all over the kitchen.

The kitchen was a disaster. It took hours to clean it up. And this was with Basil, Iris, Grandad, Goldy and me helping. It still looked pretty bad when Dad got home, and of course he immediately got worried and started shouting.

And with all the fuss and commotion nobody noticed that Gran had once again disappeared.

***

It was past eight o'clock when we sat down to supper, which was canned chili and salad. We were all really tired and cross, and it was a good thing that Gran was downstairs having a sleep — or so we thought.

111

"We just have to try and keep a better look out for Gran," Dad told us. "All of us." I guess he was pretty shaken about the fire. "We'll have to try and take turns," he said.

Then the phone started ringing, and Dad sighed and got up from the table. "Yes! Yes!" he said, as he plucked the phone off the hook.

There was a silence as he listened and then plonked the receiver down again. "Wrong number. Some woman speaking Chinese."

Grandad and I looked at one another and hurried to the basement stairs.

"Mrs. Chan?" I whispered.

"If it is, it means that ..." He didn't finish the sentence, but I knew what he meant. He meant that Gran had gone again.

And she had.

We looked all over the basement, and then I snuck upstairs and searched every room in the house. I couldn't see how Gran had managed to get away without anyone seeing her. We all thought she was having a nap.

"We won't worry your father," Grandad said

to me. "Maybe it's better he doesn't know."

That was for sure. We just had to get Gran back before Dad found out she was missing.

***

This time Iris drove Grandad and me. As we lurched around the corners, the gardening tools rattled in the back of the Green Thumb truck, and the engine shuddered in the wrong gear. I hung onto the seat belt and thought how I would rather have Grandad drive, even with his bad depth perception. I still thought he'd be safer than Iris. I also counted the days that we had left before the repo men came back to take the truck. Friday — and then Saturday.

Mrs. Chan met us at the door. She smiled at us and bowed. It was much better this time. I smiled back at her and bowed too. It was a great relief to know that we weren't going to be arrested for breaking and entering. Mrs. Chan pointed towards the basement door and made a gesture like someone piling stuff up. And that's what

Gran was doing. She was in a corner of the basement, by the furnace, surrounded by piles of old paint cans and tools.

"Hello, Josephine." Gran put down a bag of nails and smiled anxiously at me. "I'm just looking for my box ..." she stopped. "The one you gave me. I know I put it somewhere. I haven't lost it. I know I haven't."

"I know, Cessy," I smiled back. "Grandad, I mean, Arthur and I have come to take you home."

"Home?" Gran said slowly. "I am home." But she looked at the paint cans in a rather puzzled way and came upstairs with me.

Mrs. Chan had put small round cups on a table and was filling them with steaming, sweet-smelling tea. She made a sign for us to sit down.

So we sat down, even Gran, and sipped the tea and Grandad talked to Mrs. Chan in English and she talked to him in Chinese.

Gran was very quiet and kept sneaking looks at Grandad as if she wasn't at all sure who he was, and once in a while she said, "Arthur?" in a questioning sort of voice. Then, just as before, John

Chan came home, only this time he brought Iris, who had been waiting outside in the truck, and they sat down too, and Mrs. Chan made more tea and offered us all almond cookies.

It seemed that John and Iris were at the same college and even had one class together. I watched with surprise as Iris laughed and chatted with John as though she'd known him for a long time. I'd never seen Iris so talkative.

"Yes. It was a total disaster!" she laughed. "I'll have to do the whole experiment over again."

"Me too," said John. "Maybe we can do it together."

"I'd like that," said Iris, and then they smiled at each other and laughed again.

She likes him, I thought. And he likes her. I was very surprised. Iris had never had a boyfriend before, not even for her high school graduation.

Then Mrs. Chan shook John's arm and broke into a flood of Chinese.

"My grandmother wants to say she is very pleased to see you again," John translated.

"She thinks Mrs. Green has a reason for coming here. She would like to help her."

"Well, it's her memory" said Grandad, softly. "It's playing tricks."

John said something rapidly to his grandmother who shook her head and replied in what seemed to me to be a very cross voice.

"She says, no, there is something else." John shrugged. "My grandmother thinks Mrs. Green is looking for something important. She has a secret." He grinned at us. "My grandmother says she can feel it. My grandmother's a very strong-minded person."

I looked at Mrs. Chan. She seemed far too tiny to be a strong-minded person, but it was true her eyes were very bright and darted from one face to another as we talked.

***

Later, as Iris lurched us back home, I cuddled against Gran and thought about this. I didn't believe in Gran's box. But I thought Mrs. Chan might be right. Gran *was* looking for something important — her memory.

Then I started to think about how Gran got to her old house anyway. How could she get that far without any money? I yawned and closed my eyes. In spite of Iris's driving, I was falling asleep. It had been a very exhausting day.

13

Tracking Gran

FRIDAY WAS A quiet, peaceful day. This was good because Saturday turned out to be wild!

On Saturday morning I was up early as usual before anyone else. I smeared peanut butter on two pieces of toast and wandered into the garden to think.

I went over to the herb patch, which was in a sheltered spot against the back fence, and sniffed the air. Dozens of herb smells drifted up from the damp earth and surrounded me. I rubbed a sage leaf between my fingers and smelt it. Mmm! Sage smells of dry hot summer. I don't think there's a plant smell I don't like. I even like the smell of skunk cabbage. I was always amazed at how many greens there were in a row of herbs. There was the bright green crinkled leaves of the parsley, the grey-green velvet leaves of the sage, the yellow-green basil, the tiny dark green leaves of the thyme and, of course, the blue-green needles of the rosemary bush. Rosemary. The name I shared with my mum.

Somehow, I felt closer to Mum when I was standing in the herb patch. It was her favourite place in the garden. She was the one who taught me all the herb names. Mum knew a lot about herbs.

She told me that people have used herbs for thousands of years to cure diseases and keep healthy. Sage is for tooth ache, camomile is for shiny hair, parsley is for digestion, mint is for a sore throat — and rosemary is for remembrance.

Rosemary for remembrance. I picked a needle from the rosemary bush and chewed it. I didn't need any rosemary to remember Mum, but I wondered if rosemary might help Gran to remember. I picked a stalk and rubbed the needles onto the palm of my hand and put them in the pocket of my jeans. I'd try sprinkling them onto Gran's salad and see if her memory got better.

I left the herbs and wandered under the cedar branches. Suddenly I realized that I hadn't had my dream since I'd climbed the tree. And I hadn't woken up in the morning with sad feelings about Mum either. Sitting on the branch and counting the freighters must have helped somehow. I thought about this while I finished my toast and then I thought about Gran.

I was really puzzled about how Gran got to her old house. And how did she go without Grandad seeing her? I finally decided that I'd keep a constant watch on Gran for the whole weekend, and if she left for her old home again, at least I could find out how she got there.

"Well, good luck," said Grandad, when I explained what I was going to do. "Your grand-mother always gives me the slip."

I'd been puzzling about this. "I think she goes when you have your morning nap," I told him. "Gran waits until you doze off in the chair."

"I thought so too, but I just pretended to be

asleep and your Gran didn't move."

I didn't say anything, but privately I thought that Grandad probably dozed off and didn't realize it.

And that very morning I was proved right. I found a hiding spot behind the rhododendron bush by the front driveway. The first person to come past was Dad. He was all dressed up in a suit and the red-and-blue tie, and he had a briefcase under his arm. I remembered that Saturday was the day he was going to see the manager of the credit union to try to get a loan, so I held my breath and wished him all the luck in the world. Saturday was also the day that the repo men said they'd be back for the truck.

I was sheltered under the rhododendron, and the sun filtered greenly through the leaves. It was so relaxing that I almost dozed off myself. My head was nodding forward when the sound of shoes crunching on the gravel path jerked me awake. Gran, dressed in a purple fleece suit, moving with very ungranlike speed, was heading down the street to the comer.

I gave her a good start and then crept after her, silent in my running shoes. I snuck from tree to tree, pushing myself up against the bark and peering out at Gran's retreating back. I was afraid she'd look round and see me, but she stared straight ahead as though she were hypnotized.

Then I made my mistake. I didn't even think. I got to the corner house of our block and squeezed myself against the laurel hedge. That was the mistake.

"Oh, Rosemary!" a voice called, and Mrs. Dunk appeared through the front gate, with Pepi on a pink leash. "There's something I want to say to you."

Of all the bad luck. I had to run into Mrs. Dunk!

Mrs. Dunk pulled a very reluctant Pepi over to where I was flattened and shook her finger at me. She had so many rings on the finger you'd think it would fall off with the weight.

"Now," she said, and the smell of her perfume surrounded me like gas.

"About the other night."

"What about it?" I said, moving backwards and trying to hold my breath, although of course I guessed what she was going to say.

"This is a respectable neighbourhood." She pulled Pepi back from the fire hydrant. "I don't like having the police constantly down this street, and always for one family! It just won't do." I didn't say anything. There didn't seem to be anything to say.

Mrs. Dunk wagged her finger again. "That terrible flashing light from the police car shone into my bedroom window and gave both Pepi and me a migraine."

Since Pepi was jumping on my shoes and trying to bite my ankles, I didn't feel too sympathetic towards him, and I would have thought that anyone who reeked like Mrs. Dunk would have a constant headache. It was peculiar how I liked all plant smells, but Mrs. Dunk's artificial scent made me sick.

"I trust," Mrs. Dunk said sternly, "that nothing like this will occur again."

I shook my head at her and stared down the

road. Gran was disappearing around the corner. I was going to lose her.

"No, never again, Mrs. Sk...er, Dunk," I said quickly and made a run for it, leaving her with her mouth open.

I sped down the street and turned the corner, breathing hard, with a stitch in my side. But Gran had gone. My gran had just vanished into thin air!

"I don't know how she does it," said Grandad later. We were on the bus, going to pick up Gran. "It beats me."

"I even walked to the next street over," I told him. "But she'd gone all right."

"Well, it's a real puzzle" said Grandad. "Your Gran is full of surprises."

So is Grandad, I decided, later, as Mrs. Chan came to the door and Grandad said something to her in Chinese.

She put her hand over her mouth and pealed with laughter.

"What did you say, Grandad?" I plucked at his jacket. "I didn't know you could speak Chinese."

"I've been watching a Cantonese language program on TV." Grandad grinned at me. "I said 'hello,' but from the way Mrs. Chan is laughing, I don't think I got it quite right."

"Say something else," I said.

"*Ni zai ma*," Grandad said slowly.

Mrs. Chan laughed again. "*Bu shai ya*," she replied.

Grandad tried again, and this time Mrs. Chan clapped her hands and nodded.

"What did you say that time?"

"It's a nice day," said Grandad. "That's what I think I said."

Then Mrs. Chan waved us to the kitchen table, and we drank tea. Grandad and Mrs. Chan did their bowing and nodding. Grandad tried out his new Chinese words, and Mrs. Chan corrected him, and all the time we listened to Gran opening and shutting cupboards, all over the house.

"Cessy?" I went and stood beside her. "Your tea is getting cold, Cessy."

Gran smiled up at me. "Oh, Josephine." She held onto my arm and stood up. "It's somewhere ..."

She looked puzzled and stopped. "My box. It's something ... so important." She stopped again. "I must find my box."

"Never mind," I said. "Forget your box. Come and have your tea."

She let me lead her into the kitchen, where Mrs. Chan fussed over her.

We had to take the bus home because Grandad didn't have enough money for a taxi, and of course he didn't want to phone home for a ride because that would alert everyone that Gran had run away again. So, it was quite a bit later when we walked up the drive and along the side of our house.

I was pleased to see the Green Thumb truck was still outside. Maybe the repo men had forgotten all about the five days.

"Let's keep it quiet," said Grandad, one arm supporting Gran and the other fumbling for the key to the door.

I nodded at him, pushed the door gently open, and we crept inside.

There was no need to keep anything quiet.

We could have made all the noise we wanted! All the lights were on, and Dad was sitting in Grandad's easy chair, with his arms folded, and his red-and-blue tie all crooked.

"Oh! Dad!" I said in surprise. "What are you doing here?"

Dad got up and started pacing up and down the room. "Waiting," he told me.

"Ah, Brian!" Grandad helped Gran into the bedroom. "I'll just be a minute ... get Cessy tucked up for a nap. Er ... how long have you been here?"

"About three hours," Dad answered. "Ever since I saw my mother get into a car on Fourth Avenue."

"You saw Gran get into a car!" I said. "But what happened? Did she know the people in the car?"

"I'd been to the credit union to talk to the manager." Dad stopped pacing and threw himself in the chair again. "Imagine my surprise when I see my mother standing on the street corner." He paused. "So I started across the road to where she was standing."

"And?" I sort of squeaked. "And what happened? What did Gran do?"

"Do! Do! I'll tell you what your eighty-five-year-old grandmother did!" Dad's voice rose to a high-pitched howl. "She hitched a ride, that's what she did!"

"Gran hitchhiked?" I goggled at him. "She actually hitchhiked?"

"That's what she did, all right. A car came along, and she stuck out her thumb. The car stopped, and in she got." Dad threw his arms up to the ceiling. "I couldn't believe it!"

"Shhh! Cessy's trying to sleep." Grandad shut the door behind him. "She's had a tiring day."

"I'll say," I said.

"So," Grandad sat beside me, "that's how Cessy has been getting to our old house!" He gave a little chuckle. "Your grandmother is amazing."

"I'll say," I said again. I'd never have guessed that my gran was hitching rides at the street corner.

"It's no laughing matter, Father," Dad spoke sternly. "This is very serious. I suppose she went looking for her imaginary box again?"

"Well, yes," Grandad said. "But Mrs. Chan is very welcoming."

"I tried to follow the car." Dad wasn't really listening. "I ran down the road after it for blocks, waving and yelling. But it was too far ahead and I couldn't catch up with it." He sat down again. "Then I came back here and you two were gone as well."

"Mrs. Chan thinks Gran goes to the old house because she is looking for something very important," I told him.

"Her memory. That's what your gran is looking for."

"That's what I think," I said. "But Mrs. Chan thinks Gran has a secret."

Well, I don't know what," said Dad. "All I know is that it's very lucky that Mrs. Chan hasn't phoned the police."

"What would happen if she did?" I said quickly.

"She'd be charged with illegal entry!" Dad said. "If she phoned the police, your gran would be in trouble."

"That would be horrible," I shuddered at the thought of Gran being taken to the police station.

"Yes, it would," said Dad. "And hitchhiking is very dangerous. Gran is lucky that she hasn't been mugged or picked up by some loony."

That was a terrible, terrible thought. I shook my head to try not to think of it.

"And that's why we have to do something about it." Dad rubbed his hand over his eyes.

"Right away."

"Dad!" I said, and my heart started pounding in my chest as I said it. "Dad! You're not going to send Gran away are you? You're not going to..."

"Rosy! I want to talk to your grandad. I want you to go upstairs and help get dinner or something."

"But!" I was rooted to the carpet. "I want to hear what you're going to say too. I want to ..."

Dad pointed his finger at the stairs. "Rosy, please don't make this any harder for me."

"Oh, all right, but it's not fair!" I screamed the words. My voice was so loud it echoed around the room. "It's not fair!" I couldn't believe I was screaming. And I guess Grandad was surprised too because he blinked and gave me a funny look.

"Shh ... girl," he said gently. "Go on, let your Dad and me have a talk."

So I went upstairs.

"Was that you screaming, Rose?" Goldy goggled at me from the floor in front of the TV. "What's the matter?"

"Nothing you'd worry about," I said. I pushed past her, slamming the door, and flung myself on the bed.

I thought and thought, but I just couldn't find a way to help. I had secretly sprinkled the crushed rosemary leaves on Gran's salad, but it didn't seem to have any effect. At dinner I couldn't even look Gran and Grandad in the eye. It was a very quiet meal.

"Those men came for the truck," Goldy whispered to me. "They towed it away when you were in the bedroom."

"Oh," I said. I'd forgotten about the repo men and the truck. "So what!" Nothing seemed important anymore, except Gran being sent away.

It was as if we were all waiting for something, and yet nobody wanted to say what it was. I escaped as soon as I could. Dad hadn't said anything, and I was too scared to ask. Later that night I lay in bed for hours, trying to plan something, but without any success. I thought of maybe running away with Gran. But where would we go? Anyway, Gran was too old to camp out. Maybe I should have bought lottery tickets with my allowance. If I had won a million dollars, I could look after Gran myself. What had Dad decided to do? For the first time in my life I didn't want the next day to come. For the first time in my life I lay in bed and didn't want to sleep.

"Rose?" Goldy's voice came out of the dark around her bed.

"What?"

"Will we have to go on welfare now?"

"Welfare?"

"Yes. Now that the truck's gone and Dad can't do gardening. When people lose their jobs, they go on welfare. That's what some kids in my class told me. That's what happened to their families."

"Maybe the credit union will let Dad have the loan," I said.

"The manager said he'd go through the Green Thumb accounts and let Dad know on Monday."

"Did you hear Dad say that?"

"I heard him tell Grandad. Grandad said that sounded 'iffy.' What's 'iffy' mean?"

I didn't answer. I didn't care. All I could think about was Gran. And after a while Goldy stopped talking and fell asleep. I lay awake, listening to the funny little snuffling sounds coming from her bed. Even in her sleep Goldy sounded as if she was telling stories!

The glow from my night light was yellow and soothing, and out of the window I could see a new moon like a slice of lemon hanging over the mountains. It was strange, but the night no longer seemed so terrifying. And then I thought maybe if I stayed awake all night, like a vigil, if I kept a watch all night, some sort of miracle might happen, and my gran wouldn't be sent away.

I stared at the lemon moon. I thought about my mum and cried. I thought about Gran and cried some more. Then I thought about Dad getting caught in the burglar trap and I giggled. It was really odd one moment to have such sad thoughts and be crying and the next moment to have such funny thoughts and be laughing. And then I thought that maybe this is what life is like. Sad and funny all muddled together.

Little jigsaw bits of ideas drifted through my head. I tried to get them to fit together. I tried to stay awake, but I couldn't.

14

Hide and Seek

BRIGHT SUNDAY SUNLIGHT was streaming in the window when I opened my eyes. The clock radio on the bedside table said nine-thirty! I had never slept that late in my entire life.

"Where is everyone?" Goldy was the only one in the kitchen, and the house seemed very quiet and still.

"Out!" Goldy said briefly, her mouth full of cereal. "Boy, did you sleep in. You're the last one up. It's taken me ages to find the cereal. I could have died of starvation. But guess what? I found the jam and the toothpaste too."

"Out where?" I said.

"How should I know?" She crunched steadily.

"Well, you must know something!" I felt like smacking her.

"All I know is that Dad and Grandad went to catch a bus." Goldy looked peeved. "They said I couldn't go with them."

"Well, where were they going?" I said, my throat feeling very dry.

"I don't know. They didn't say. But Dad had a list of something called ..." She stopped and thought. "I've forgotten."

"Goldy!" I sat down beside her. "Please. Please. Try and remember. It's very important."

"Nobody tells me anything." Goldy complained. "But I think we're going to move."

"Move?" I said.

"Well, Dad's list was all about homes they were going to see," said Goldy.

"Nursing homes. Was that it?" I asked, but I already knew the answer.

She nodded. "Yes, that's it. I think we are going to move, Rose. Dad's going to sell this house, and we're going to move to the country where it's a lot cheaper to live. We're going to have an extra-large house with a swimming pool and a tower with a flag, and I'm going to have the top room in the tower."

"Sure, Goldy," I said, and then the phone rang.

"It's for you." Goldy handed over the receiver. "Some weird woman ... keeps saying, 'Rosee! Rosee!'"

"Hello," I said. "This is Rose Green speaking."

"Rosee! Rosee! *Ni zai ma*?" A high-pitched voice shouted in my ear, and then a whole flood of Cantonese. "Rose ... Come!"

It was Mrs. Chan. Gran must have gone home again.

"I'm coming, Mrs. Chan," I shouted back. "I'll come as quick as I can."

"Rosee! Rosee! Come!" Mrs. Chan repeated.

"Yes! All right. I'm coming!" I shouted again and then I hung up. I wasn't sure whether Mrs. Chan understood or not, but I couldn't waste time saying the same thing over and over. I had to get Gran back before Dad returned.

If Dad found out that Gran had run away again he'd never change his mind about the nursing home. There'd be no hope at all.

"Where's Basil and Iris?" I yelled at Goldy as I pulled on my jeans and T-shirt. "I need some money for the bus."

"Out," said Goldy, following me into the bathroom and watching me comb my hair. "Basil is playing basketball and Iris has gone off to the library with that John guy. I think she's keen on him." She swung on the door handle.

"Why do you want money for the bus? Where are you going? What's happening?"

I didn't answer her. "Have you got any money? I'll pay you back."

"You always say that, but you never do." She folded her arms. "I'm not lending you any more. So there."

"You have to!" I grabbed the sleeve of her housecoat. "I've got to go and get Gran, and I've got to get her back here before Dad gets back."

"Why?" Goldy said. "Tell me."

"Oh, don't argue!" I pulled her along the hall to our room. "Just get me the money."

"No!" Goldy dug in her heels and held onto the door frame. "No way."

"I'll just have to take it then," I said, and I thrust her away from me and made a dive for her piggy bank on the dresser.

"You can't do that!" Goldy grabbed me and tried to snatch the piggy bank back. "It's my money and my pig. You're stealing." She kicked my shins. "I'm telling."

"It's an emergency!" I pushed her onto the bed. "Be quiet!"

"Give that back!" She lunged at me again as I reached the door and grabbed my arm. The pig slipped from my grasp and crashed to the floor.

Hundreds of little pieces smashed in all directions.

"You've broken my pig!" Goldy hit out at me.

"I'm sorry." I bent down and picked up two loonies. "I'll get you a new one."

"I don't want a new one. I want that one!" Goldy wailed as I pulled away and made a break for the front door.

I raced down the hill, the laces of my untied sneakers flapping as I ran. My thoughts were so knotted that my head ached.

"Rose! Wait for me!" a voice screeched from behind me. "Wait for me!" It was Goldy, running after me in her quilted pink housecoat and fluffy slippers.

"Go home!" I shouted back over my shoulder. "Go home, Goldy. Don't be so stupid."

"Don't leave me!" Goldy screeched louder. "I'm all alone in the house. Don't leave me alone!"

I stopped and turned around. And there was Mrs. Dunk, her arms folded, standing on her front porch, staring. "Will you two girls stop all that shouting," she hissed at us. "It's Sunday morning. It's supposed to be a day of rest. And that means quiet!"

I groaned. She'd complain to Dad. What bad luck, and what a nuisance Goldy was.

"All right," I sighed, as Goldy slid and slipped up to me. "You can come with me. But we have to hurry."

"I've never been out in my housecoat before." Goldy padded along beside me. "People may think I'm escaping from being kidnapped. They may think that my father is a billionaire and the kidnappers want a gigantic ransom for me."

I didn't want to, but I had to grin. You just couldn't keep Goldy down. She was like one of those fat toy men that you knock over and they just bounce back.

***

I looked out the window of the trolley bus. The sun had disappeared. Large drops of rain were spotting the glass. I hadn't brought a raincoat.

The bus was crammed full. All the seats were taken, and we had to grab onto the seat backs to stop from falling as the bus swayed round corners. The smell of dozens of different bodies and their steaming raincoats made me wrinkle my nose. I could hardly see out of the window because of the steam, and I worried about changing buses. I knew we had to change to the North Shore bus at Georgia Street, but how would I know when the bus got there? I'd never been on the bus without an adult before.

"People are staring at me!" Goldy hissed in my ear.

I looked down at her housecoat and fuzzy slippers. No wonder.

"That teenager with the purple hair keeps laughing!" Goldy hung onto me as the bus jerked forward.

I snuck a look around. It was true. This skinny teenager with a purple mohawk was killing himself giggling and pointing at Goldy. You'd think a purple-haired punk would have more sense than to laugh at someone just because she was wearing her housecoat and slippers. The bus pulled up at a stop. It must be a transfer stop, I thought as I watched a rush of people scurrying for the exit, and I pushed Goldy into an empty seat and sank down across from her.

"You're in the handicapped seat." A voice by my ear made me jump.

"What?" I stared at the old man sitting next to me. He was sitting very straight with a cane between his legs.

"I said, you're in the handicapped seat. You should let that lady sit down."

I looked around and saw a pregnant woman holding onto an overhead strap.

"Oh, I'm sorry." I felt my face burning. I stood up. "I didn't ..."

"Thank you," said the woman and eased herself down into the seat. "It's hard on the legs being pregnant."

"Yes," I said, but I can't say I'd ever thought about such a thing.

"Kids!" said the old man and made a face.

I felt my face burn hotter.

"She didn't mean it," Goldy said loudly, defending me.

"Don't mind him," said the woman, winking at me. "He's just a grouch."

"Yes," I said, not really listening, twisting my head left and right. I was trying to catch a glimpse through the steamy windows. Where were we? We were lost. We should have stayed home. We should have waited for Dad. Now what were we going to do?

"Where are you getting off?" said the woman, smiling at me, breaking into my thoughts. Maybe she could see I was nervous.

"Georgia Street." I swallowed. Now I was talking to a stranger. Dad had forbidden us ever to speak to strangers. There are real nut cases out there, he'd said. But surely a pregnant woman wasn't a nut case?

"Me too," said the woman.

"Oh really!" I took a deep breath. And suddenly the whole bus looked more friendly. "What are you going to call your baby?" I asked.

"James or Jennifer," laughed the woman. "Whichever fits." And she leaned up to pull the cord. "Here we are."

It was at this point that I remembered I hadn't asked the bus driver for transfers.

"Oh, no!" I grabbed Goldy's hand, and we pushed our way frantically to the front of the bus.

"Sorry," said the driver, shaking his head and blaring the trolley horn at a car that was trying to cut in ahead of him. "You have to get your transfers when you get on."

"I forgot," I said. I felt desperate.

"Sorry," repeated the driver.

"Oh, please, just this once," I begged him. "I'll never forget again. We're going to get our grandmother. We have to take her back home, and we only just have enough money." I looked at him. "She's eighty-five years old." I didn't know why I said this, but it was definitely the right thing to say.

"Oh, all right," the driver punched a button and with a sharp buzz, the machine printed two transfers and dropped them into a metal tray. The driver scooped them up and handed them to me. "Just this once. I'm a sucker for eighty-five-year-old grandmothers." And he laughed. We hopped off the trolley bus, and I skipped to the transfer stop. Even the rain dripping down my neck didn't stop me feeling triumphant, as though I had done something really clever.

***

Goldy shuffled up behind me as I pressed the door bell.

"We'll get Gran and take her right back home." I could hear footsteps coming to the door.

"If we're quick no one will know she's been gone."

"But how will we get home?" Goldy said. "We don't have any money left."

I turned and stared at her. Why hadn't I thought of that?

But then the front door opened, and Mrs. Chan was bowing us inside and talking very fast.

"What's she saying?" Goldy whispered as we followed her to the kitchen.

"I don't know." I shrugged my shoulders. "But I expect she is ..." I stopped in mid-sentence.

Gran was in the middle of the kitchen surrounded by towering piles of cans, bottles, sauce-pans, and dishes. All the cupboard doors were open, and the cupboards were empty.

"Wow!" Goldy hissed. "What is going on? Gran, what are you doing?"

"Goldy, I don't think she's going to know you today," I said quickly. "Don't get mad."

"Josephine!" Gran looked up. "Have you come to help?"

"Hello, Cessy," I picked my way across the

room. "Sure. What shall I do?"

"I'm looking for my box." Gran smiled at me. "And this lady," she waved towards Mrs. Chan, "has very kindly offered to help me."

Mrs. Chan and I bowed to one another, and Mrs. Chan beamed at Gran.

"You can help search through the cupboards," Gran said, "And your little friend can help too if she wants." Gran smiled at Goldy.

"I'm Goldy," Goldy said.

"Come on, little friend," I whispered to her as I opened a cupboard door. "The sooner we search, the sooner we can get Gran to go home." Even as I said the words, I realized we were stuck unless John Chan came back from the library.

"I wish I'd stayed home by myself now," grumbled Goldy. "I could have locked all the doors and windows and watched TV."

Half an hour later I was ready to agree with Goldy. The kitchen looked like a cross between a supermarket and a garbage dump. Mrs. Chan had got a three-step ladder and was taking everything out of the top cupboards. Gran had cleared the bottom ones, and Goldy and I were taking all the stuff out of the drawers. It looked as if we'd never finish, and time was rushing past us. I couldn't help looking round every minute or so in case John's parents appeared. For all I knew they could be still in bed or at church or out for a Sunday morning walk. And if they appeared would Mrs. Chan be able to explain what was going on? Had she even told them about Gran coming over? I had the feeling that she hadn't. They'd probably phone the police.

Also, I was starving. I hadn't had breakfast and my stomach was so empty it felt like a big hole inside me. My tummy was gurgling and rumbling like some churning cement mixer.

Mrs. Chan must have heard it because she opened the fridge and took out a plate of yellow pastry tarts. She pointed to the plate and then to me. I could understand that all right. I wolfed down one and then two — they were so good that I couldn't stop — but Mrs. Chan didn't seem to mind. She patted her stomach and nodded at me, so I ate another one.

I licked my fingers and watched Gran scuttling from cupboard to cupboard. "My box! My box!" she whispered over and over. "It's here. I know it is."

Poor Gran. Nobody believed in her box. Well, nobody except Mrs. Chan. I looked at Mrs. Chan. She was back up on a chair carefully searching the top shelves. And I wondered why John's gran was so sure about my gran. They didn't even speak the same language. But Mrs. Chan chose to believe Gran, and the rest of us chose not to. And that meant me too. I was choosing not to believe Gran. And I suddenly felt very bad. It was true that all the things that Gran had done seemed crazy, but that didn't mean I shouldn't trust her.

I hurried across the kitchen floor, stepping over piles of boxes and cans. "Gran! Cessy!"

I put my hand on her arm. "I really believe in your box. I really do. Don't worry. We'll find it."

"Josephine!" My gran smiled at me, such a sweet smile. "I know the box is here, somewhere. If I could just remember ..."

"Well, let's think," I said, smiling back at her. I thought of all the things Gran had done to try and find her box: She'd had me dig up the rose bushes and climb the cedar tree. She'd collected all the umbrellas and cut up a blue-velvet cushion. None of this made sense, but if I was going to believe Gran I had to trust her.

"Cessy, listen," I said. "Listen to this: roses, cedar, umbrellas, blue velvet. What do they mean?"

But Gran didn't listen. She bent down and started rummaging through another drawer.

"Cessy!" I squatted beside her. "Please, listen." I spoke louder. "Cedar, roses, blue velvet, umbrellas." I caught Gran's hand and held it tight. Her skin was downy soft and creased with thousands of small wrinkles. "Roses, cedar, blue velvet, umbrellas. Roses, cedar, blue velvet, umbrellas."

I said the words over and over.

Gran started to pull her hand away impatiently, but then she stopped. Her hand quivered and lay still in mine.

"Cedar, blue velvet, roses, umbrellas," I chanted. "Your box, Cessy. Your box."

Gran held onto the counter with her free hand and slowly pulled herself up. "Yes," she said, almost to herself. "Umbrellas …"

15

Discovery!

THERE WAS A long silence. From somewhere a clock struck twelve. Goldy was breathing hard like a busy engine. Mrs. Chan had got off her chair and had her hands clasped together.

"Yes," said Gran again. "Yes. Yes ..." And she pulled her hand away and hurried out of the kitchen, across the living room carpet and into the hall.

We scurried after her, crowding into the tiny hallway.

Gran was standing by the coat rack. "My box!" she said, and her voice became all happy and full of laughter."

"Is there really a box, Rose?" Goldy hissed at me.

"Shh!" I said, watching Gran.

"But where is it then?" Goldy tugged at my sleeve. "I can't see a box. There isn't any box."

I didn't answer her. I was watching Gran as she bent down and pulled at the black metal umbrella tray at the bottom of the rack.

"What is it? What's Gran doing?" Goldy tried to push me out of the way so she could see better.

"Stop it, Goldy." I pushed her back, my eyes fixed on Gran.

Gran lifted up the metal tray. There was a narrow space underneath and hidden inside this space was a thin wooden box. A cedar box covered with carved roses!

"There *is* a box!" Goldy gave a little scream. "Gran did have a box!"

"Yes!" I took such a deep, gulping breath I felt giddy.

Mrs. Chan started clapping her hands.

Gran straightened up and held out the box to me.

I grabbed it.

"What's inside? What's inside?" Goldy was

jumping up and down and stepping on my toes.

What could be inside the box that was so important? I tugged at the lid.

"Open it! Open it!" Goldy was squeaking in her excitement.

"I'm trying!" I said. I pulled at the lid and pried it. But the lid wouldn't open.

"There's a key hole!" Goldy was breathing into my face. "Give it to me!" And she tugged the box from my grasp.

"But no key!" I stumbled over the words.

"Give it back to me!"

It was at just this moment that the back door opened with a crash, and voices called out from the porch.

Mrs. Chan made a little clucking sound and hurried away. I ran after her.

It was John Chan's mother and father with armloads of groceries, trying to get into the kitchen.

Well, they tried to get in, but a pile of cans was in the way of the door, and John's father tripped over the cans and his grocery bags flew out of his arms and crashed across the floor. Lettuces and tomatoes skidded and squished over the tiles and an orange puddle began flowing round them.

After this things got very mixed up. Mrs. Chan burst into a flood of Cantonese and ran forward with a dish towel trying to shoo John's parents out of the way as if they were chickens that had wandered. It didn't take too much brainwork to guess immediately that she hadn't told the Chans anything about Gran.

By the looks on their faces they seemed a bit stunned. I guess all the strange people plus the state of the kitchen and the wrecked groceries would be enough to bewilder anyone.

Gran seemed quite bewildered too. She sat in a chair clutching her box and looking as if she didn't really believe she was in the kitchen of her old house.

"Let's get out of here!" Goldy hissed at me. "We're going to get into trouble." She started tugging me towards the door.

I didn't know what to do. If it was just Goldy

and me, we would have a chance. We could cut through the living room and out the front door and maybe hide in someone's garden. But we couldn't leave Gran.

"We can't leave Gran here alone," I whispered back. "What if they take her to the police station? We have to stay with her."

"Yeah. I guess," Goldy let go of my sleeve.

"I wish I'd read the Sunday comics."

"What?"

"They might not let us read them in jail,"she said. "I expect they'd only let us read serious papers, not the funnies."

"We're not going to jail!" I gave her a bit of a shove. "We're children. Children don't go to jail."

"I guess not," Goldy said, sounding disappointed.

Just then, John's mother sort of hopped over the mess on the floor and came and stood next to us. She smelt of jasmine. "My name is Mai-Lan Chan," she said, "and this is my husband, Kenneth." She waved at John's father, who was picking up bits of tomato and listening to Mrs. Chan's excited speech. "Would you like to tell us who you are?"

"I'm Rose, this is my sister, Goldy, and this is our grandmother," I said, and I stared at the floor.

"Ah! Your grandmother!" Mai-Lan went over to Gran and shook her hand. "My mother-in-law tells us that this used to be your house."

I held my breath. What would Gran say? Would she ask Mai-Lan to leave?

Gran stroked the roses on the cedar box very gently and then looked up at Mai-Lan Chan. "Yes,"she said, very clearly. "I used to live here. I'm sorry. I hid this box away ..." She stopped. "I forgot. I forgot where I had put it." She looked puzzled. "I hid the box to keep it safe."

I let my breath out in a great rush. I was so relieved. Gran had zapped back into GD form. It must have been finding the box.

Then Kenneth Chan came over and shook Gran's hand and smiled at Goldy and me — and then he thanked us. My head began to swirl around. He actually thanked us. They weren't going to send for the police at all.

"My mother loves a secret," he said. He turned to Mrs. Chan and said something in Cantonese, and she laughed. "My mother did not want to come to Canada. She was happy living with my brother in Hong Kong, but she had to come to live with us when my brother moved to England. She has been very miserable, but then a few weeks ago she suddenly got a lot more cheerful. We didn't know why. We didn't know she had secret visitors."

"My mother-in-law has even started to learn English!" Mai-Lan Chan said, smiling at us. "She said she would never, never learn any English, but now she is watching the Cantonese-English lessons on TV."

"So, we are very happy about this." Kenneth Chan nodded at his mother.

Then Mrs. Chan grabbed the sleeve of his suit and said something very fast.

"Ah!" Kenneth Chan said. "My mother is afraid that now the grandmother has found her box, she will never see you again."

Mrs. Chan nodded.

Gran turned to me. "Is that right, Rose? Have I been coming here a lot?"

"Yes, Gran," I said. "Nearly every day." I didn't know what else to say.

"I see," Gran said, slowly. "And do you know how I got here? Did your grandad bring me here?"

"No, Gran," I said. "You hitchhiked."

"I hitchhiked," Gran repeated the words. "Well," she gave a little smile. "I haven't done that since World War II." But she didn't sound too unhappy about it. She sort of straightened up in the chair. Then she looked up at Kenneth Chan. "It sounds as if your mother has been very good to me. Would you thank her and tell her that of course I will still see her. Maybe she can come to visit us."

***

So that was all right. And right afterwards I said we just had to get home and so Mai-Lan Chan drove us in her black car. With any luck we would get back before Dad and Grandad, and no one would know we had even left.

But that didn't happen. When we pulled up outside our house even the cloud of rain didn't stop me seeing that the house was lit up like a Christmas tree. We had definitely been missed.

16

Is It Too Late?

I DIDN'T KNOW what to do. As we got out of the car Dad ran down the front steps with an umbrella. He'd obviously been pulling his beard a lot, because it stuck out in all directions.

Well!" he cried, holding the umbrella over Gran's head. "Well! Going off and leaving all the doors wide open! What were you all thinking of?" Then he caught sight of Goldy in her housecoat. "What ..."

"Well, what, Brian?" Gran said calmly. "Let me introduce you to Mai-Lan Chan. We have been visiting at the old house."

I just hugged myself. Gran sounded like her old self. Finding the box had really put her in GD form all right.

I wish I'd had a camera to take a picture of Dad's face. His mouth opened so wide with surprise and he just ran right out of words.

"Uh —! Er —! Hi!" he finally managed to say to Mai-Lan, who smiled at him.

"We'll expect to see you soon, Mrs. Green," Mai-Lan called out the window of her car as as it moved slowly away from the curb.

"And Mr. Green, of course. And Rose and Goldy, if they'd like to visit." And the car swept off in a swish of wet tires and spray.

"A very nice family," said Gran as she held onto Dad's arm to climb the steps. "And I found my lost box," she added.

"Yes, Mother," Dad said.

I jumped up the steps two at a time. Now Dad would see that Gran was just fine, and they could forget about looking at nursing homes. At least that's what I thought.

Grandad was sitting at the kitchen table drinking coffee, surrounded by piles of brochures and papers. I could see right away that one of the brochures said, WEBSTER'S REST HOME in big print. I grabbed it off the table. "Extended care facility," I read. "Three meals a day, laundry, extensive grounds, twenty-four-hour care ..."

"That seemed the best of the bunch." Grandad gave me a little smile, and then got up to put his arm around Gran. "They'd give us a nice double room, and we could even take a few pieces of our furniture."

"You're not going too, Grandad?" I said. "You'd hate it!" I had never thought that Grandad might go as well.

"You don't think I'd let your Gran go by herself, do you?" he said. "After being nagged for sixty-five years I'm a bit addicted to it." He grinned at Gran.

"I don't understand, Arthur." Gran looked at him. "What is all this?"

"I told you, Cessy, that we were going to move," Grandad replied softly.

"Did you?" she said.

"It's a very nice place, Mother," Dad said earnestly, nodding. "You'll like it. You won't have to worry about anything. And they will give you special care."

"But I don't want to move," said Gran, looking from one to the other. "I like it here, and Arthur likes it here, and now that I've found my box I don't have to worry anymore."

And she handed the box to Dad.

"Yes. Well." Dad coughed. "Thank you. Mum It's very nice."

"Open it!" Gran said, sitting down at the table. "Go on! Open it!"

"What's inside it. Gran?" I said.

"Wait and see," she said, nodding at Dad encouragingly.

"But it's locked," said Dad.

"I've lost the key. You'll have to break it open,' Gran said firmly. "Or do you want me to do it?"

"No!" Dad said hurriedly "I'll do it." I don't think he wanted Gran using sharp tools. He got a knife from the drawer and forced it into the crack.

Everyone was crowded around behind him looking over his shoulder, trying to peer into the box.

"Ahhh!" Dad said, as the lid opened.

17

Gran's Lost Box

Rainbows flashed and glinted into the air. I let my breath out with a sigh. Diamonds. Great Aunt Josephine's diamond earrings. I recognized them right away. The diamond earrings in the photo of my Great Aunt Josephine. Two shining diamond earrings — nestled like dewdrops in a lupine — on a bed of blue velvet!

Dad held the blue velvet up so we could all see, and the jewels glinted and sparkled as if they had caught fire.

"There," said Gran, with satisfaction. "It's for you, Brian. Josephine's earrings. She left the earrings to me in her will. You can sell them and get out of debt." She patted his hand. "And now I'm feeling a little tired. I'm going to put my feet up for a bit." She walked carefully across the room and down the stairs.

Everyone began to talk at once. I couldn't tell if Dad was going to laugh or cry. Grandad just kept nodding and saying, "GD form. That's my Cessy," over and over. Goldy was talking to everyone, and no one was listening to anyone.

"But Grandad," I pulled at his sleeve. "How come you didn't know about the earrings? Didn't Gran tell you she was hiding them?"

Grandad grinned at me. "I've been thinking about that. It seems to me that your Gran must have hidden them when she came back from her sister's funeral. You remember, she forgot she was staying here and went back to our old house. I think she hid them to keep them safe."

"And then she forgot what she'd done!" I said.

"That's what I'm thinking."

"And you didn't know about the secret hiding place?"

"No!" Grandad laughed. "Your Gran likes to have a few secrets."

"Just like Mrs. Chan," I said.

"Just like Mrs. Chan," Grandad agreed.

***

How did it all turn out? Unfortunately, Great Aunt Josephine's earrings didn't make us rich. The diamond earrings looked very dazzling, but when they were sold, they only got us just enough money to get the truck back from the repo men. Getting the truck back was good, but we were still broke. However, Dad did get a phone call from the manager of the credit union to say he'd got the loan. Thank goodness! Green Thumb Gardeners was able to get back into business and Dad was able to afford someone to come into the house for a few hours a day and help look after Gran. So Gran didn't have to go to the nursing home after all.

***

Gran continued to have GDs and BDs, and after

a while I persuaded Dad to forget he was Brian on Gran's BDs and to call himself something else. So he did.

"I'm Napoleon," he tells her now. This makes him laugh so I figure that's better than getting upset.

Once she'd found the box, Gran stopped running away. She still puts clothes in the freezer and things like that, but Mrs. O'Riley keeps an eye on Gran and makes sure she doesn't leave the taps turned on, or do anything dangerous.

"Now, Rosy," Dad said to me. "One day Gran may get so she needs a lot more nursing care and then she will have to move to a special nursing home."

I nodded. "But that's in the future," I said.

Gran and Grandad go and visit Mrs. Chan, and John Chan brings his grandmother to see us. This is very interesting, because John and Iris see each other all the time, and I caught Iris looking at pictures of wedding gowns in a magazine! If they get married then we will be related to Mrs. Chan — and I will have another gran.